HOUDINI AND ME

DAN GUTMAN
HOUDINI AND ME

HOLIDAY HOUSE is registered in the U.S. Patent and Trademark Office.

Printed and bound in November 2020 at Maple Press, York, PA, USA.

www.holidayhouse.com

First Edition

1 3 5 7 9 10 8 6 4 2

Library of Congress Cataloging-in-Publication Data

Names: Gutman, Dan, author.
Title: Houdini and me / Dan Gutman.
Description: New York City : Holiday House, 2021. | Audience: Ages 8–12.
Audience: Grades 4–6. | Summary: Eleven-year-old Harry Mancini lives in the
house where Houdini spent his final years, so he has always been interested
in the famous magician, and has even learned a few simple magic tricks; he
just never expected Houdini to contact him from beyond the grave—and what
Houdini wants him to do could well cost Harry his own life.
Identifiers: LCCN 2019049888 | ISBN 9780823445158 (hardcover)
Subjects: LCSH: Houdini, Harry, 1874–1926—Juvenile fiction. | Escape
artists—Juvenile fiction. | Near-death experiences—Juvenile fiction.
Identity (Psychology)—Juvenile fiction. | Paranormal fiction. | CYAC:
Houdini, Harry, 1874–1926—Fiction. | Escape artists—Fiction. | Near-death
experiences—Fiction. | Identity—Fiction. | Supernatural—Fiction.
LCGFT: Paranormal fiction.
Classification: LCC PZ7.G9846 Hr 2021 | DDC 813.54 [Fic]—dc23
LC record available at https://lccn.loc.gov/2019049888

ISBN: 978-0-8234-4515-8 (hardcover)

Thanks to: Amy Toth, Dr. Scott Kolander,
Elizabeth Law, Eryn Levine, Howard Wolf,
John Simko, Lauren Nicole, Lisa Lee,
Nina Wallace, Peter Lerangis, Ray Dimetrosky,
and the Houdini Museum in New York City.

*"I am perfectly willing to believe,
my mind is wide open."*
—Harry Houdini

THE GREAT MANCINI

I was born in Harry Houdini's house.

I didn't just say that so you'd keep reading. I said it because it's true.

You don't have to believe me. If I wasn't me, I wouldn't believe me either. But it's true, I swear. Look, I took this picture of the plaque outside my front door.

I live on West 113th Street in New York City. If you don't know New York that well,

HOUDINI

1874-1926

The magician lived here from 1904 to 1926,
collecting illusions, theatrical memorabilia,
and books on psychic phenomena and magic.
Famous for daring escapes,
no restraints-ropes, chains, straitjackets,
bank vaults, or jail cells-could hold him.

HISTORIC LANDMARKS PRESERVATION
CENTER

113th Street is just three blocks from the most famous park in the world—Central Park. My house is right at the beginning of Harlem.

Anyway, this is where I was born and where I've lived all my eleven years. That's right, I wasn't born in a hospital. It's a long story that I won't bore you with, but my parents weren't able to get to the hospital in time, so I was born right here on 113th Street. I wonder if my folks saved money on hospital bills.

A century ago, this was Harry Houdini's house. He lived here for the last twenty-two years of his life.

Most likely, you know Houdini's name, but you probably don't know all that much about him. He was a famous magician and illusionist, but he was *most* famous for being an escape artist. They would lock him up in handcuffs, in a jail cell, a rolltop desk, a giant milk can, and a mailbag. He was even locked inside a hot-water heater!

He'd always find a way to get out. A Chicago envelope company once sealed him inside the world's largest envelope. He escaped. Houdini even escaped from inside a giant football.

They could lock him up in just about *anything* and he would find a way to get out. There was nobody else like him. A century ago, Harry Houdini was one of the most famous people in the world.

When I walk up the stairs in my house, it's cool to think that Houdini walked up those same stairs. When I go down to the basement, it's the same basement where Houdini practiced his escapes. When I go to sleep at night,

I'm sleeping in a room where Harry Houdini might have slept. When I get up in the morning, I step on a floorboard next to my bed that makes a loud creaking sound that Houdini might have heard when he lived in the house a hundred years ago.

Living in the house once owned by this famous guy, I naturally became curious about him. I've read a bunch of biographies and learned a lot. To be completely honest, I'm sort of obsessed with Houdini, and with magic.

People walking past my house are always stopping to take pictures of the plaque on the wall and asking me questions about Houdini. It makes me feel like I'm a little famous too. I like that.

Oh, I forgot to tell you. The funny thing is, my name is Harry too. My parents didn't name me after Houdini. They just liked the name. And my last name is Mancini, which sounds a lot like Houdini. Mancini is an Italian name. Houdini wasn't Italian. In fact, he wasn't even born with the name Houdini.

Harry Houdini's *real* name was Erik Weisz.

He was a Jewish kid who was born in Budapest, Hungary. His family came to America and lived in Wisconsin before they moved to New York City when Erik was a teenager.

Growing up, Erik's idol was a French magician named Robert-Houdin. Harry just added an "i" to the end of "Houdin" and called himself "Houdini" for the rest of his life. I don't know why he changed his name from Erik to Harry. I guess he thought "Harry Houdini" sounded better than "Erik Houdini."

Lots of kids from school have seen the plaque on the wall, of course, so everybody knows I live in Houdini's house. Sometimes they ask me to do magic tricks, so I learned a few.

You know how grown-ups always say, "Don't try this at home, kids"? Well here's a really simple magic trick you can try at home to impress your friends. All you need is a raw egg, a little salt, and a smooth, level table.

First, challenge your friends to try to balance the egg on its end so it stands up all by itself. It's really hard to do, and they probably won't be able to do it.

Now here's the trick—while your friends are trying to balance the egg (and not looking at you), take a little pinch of salt in one hand. Wave your other hand above the table and say some magic mumbo jumbo like "abracadabra" or "hocus-pocus." While they're watching that hand, use your other to put the pinch of salt on the table.

This is called "misdirection," and it's the key to many magic tricks. Magicians get you to watch one thing so you don't notice something else they're doing at the same time.

Anyway, build a *tiny* mound of salt on the table with your fingers. Just a few grains will be enough to form a little base that will hold up the egg, the same way a tee holds up a football for a kickoff. Position the egg on top of the salt until the egg stands up. Then quietly blow away any extra grains of salt.

Presto! You've done it, as if by magic. For the fun of it, tell your friends some more mumbo jumbo about how the position of the sun and the moon on that particular date make it possible to make an egg stand up on one end. That's garbage, of course, but it *sounds* like it makes sense.

It's pretty cool to see the look on your friends' faces when the egg stands up by itself. Maybe I'll be a magician when I grow up. My best friend, Zeke Austin, already calls me "The Great Mancini."

Houdini was a really mysterious guy, so naturally there are rumors that my house is haunted. In fact, the lady who owned the house after Houdini died was convinced there was buried treasure in the basement. She spent a year digging around down there, but she never found anything.

People make up crazy stuff like that all the time. Like at my school, kids are always saying the boys' bathroom on the second floor is haunted. They probably say the same thing about the bathroom in your school. Kids always say weird stuff to try to freak people out.

The thing is, when Houdini was alive, a lot of people believed that he had supernatural powers. He did such amazing things that people couldn't believe he was just doing tricks.

For instance, he would be handcuffed, shackled, and locked in a big wooden trunk that would then be thrown into a river. It looked like he was sure to drown and die a horrible death. Then, a few minutes later, he would pop up to the surface with no handcuffs or shackles on him. The trunk was still locked and sealed. Nobody knew how Houdini got out. The only explanation seemed to be that he could make the atoms of his body dematerialize and then rematerialize outside the box. People thought that he must have had superpowers. That nothing could kill him.

Well, they thought that until Houdini actually *did* die for real, on Halloween night in 1926. But even after his death, people were convinced that he would somehow find a way to come back from the dead. To this day, every Halloween, mediums all over the world hold séances to try to communicate with the spirit of Houdini.

When he was alive, Houdini never claimed to have supernatural powers. He insisted that he was just doing tricks. But he also said something else. He told his wife Bess that after he died, if there was any way for him to come back from the dead and communicate with her, he would do it. If *anybody* could come back from the dead, it would be Harry Houdini.

I never thought too much about any of that creepy stuff. A house is just a house, right? It doesn't matter who lived in it a hundred years ago. There's no such thing as ghosts, and the living can't communicate with the dead.

But then one day something happened that changed my mind. And my life. I'll tell you the whole story.

THE FREEDOM TUNNEL

Riverside Park is a long, thin strip next to the Hudson River. It's just five blocks from my house. Hidden underneath the park is a tunnel that's nearly three miles long. It's called the Freedom Tunnel. Back in the 1980s the train line that went through the tunnel was shut down for a while, and a bunch of homeless people and graffiti artists set up a tent city down there. They were called the Mole People.

Hardly anybody knows about the Freedom Tunnel. Well, I know about it. My best friend Zeke knows about it. And now you know about it. But pretty much nobody else does. Iron gates cover the archways now to prevent people from going onto the tracks and getting run over by trains.

Zeke and I hang out in Riverside Park all the time after school. (His full name is Ezekiel but everybody calls him Zeke.) Zeke is African American and I'm white. I don't know why

I'm bothering to tell you that, but just in case you're interested, that's who we are.

Anyway, Zeke and I were hanging out near the Freedom Tunnel one day after school and complaining about our parents, which is what we usually complain about. Zeke was saying that his parents wouldn't let him play some video game because they think it's too violent.

"I told 'em that playing violent video games is a great way to blow off steam," Zeke explained. "That way, kids don't become violent in real life. But they weren't buying it."

I only have my mom. My dad died a long time ago. I was complaining that my mom won't let me have my own cell phone. Everybody else in fifth grade has a cell phone except me. My mom says that if I had a phone I'd spend my whole day staring at the screen instead of interacting with the real world. When I tell her that's not gonna happen, she comes up with other reasons why I can't have my own phone: I'll lose it, or there's inappropriate stuff online, or companies will be able to track me and invade my privacy. You know, all the usual reasons parents don't want their kids to have phones.

I have to admit she's probably right about that stuff, but I still want a phone! All my friends have one. I told Mom that I need one so I can reach her in case of an emergency, but she wasn't falling for that. Everybody knows that when you get a phone for emergencies, you end up using it to text goofy pictures and stuff to your friends.

"Hey, are you coming to my birthday party?" Zeke asked me out of the blue.

"When is it?"

"Next Thursday," he told me. "I e-mailed you an invite. Didn't you get it? You didn't reply."

"I didn't check my e-mail."

"You need to get a smartphone, dude," Zeke told me. "Join the 21st century."

"I know."

"It's an escape-room party," Zeke said.

"Escape rooms are lame," I replied, even though I had never been to an escape room and had no idea what they were like.

"No, this one is supposed to be cool," Zeke told me. "They lock you up in a dungeon and you have to figure out how to open a bunch of locks to get out. Just like your man, Houdini. C'mon, it'll be fun."

"Okay, I guess I'll go," I replied.

Suddenly a train roared through the Freedom Tunnel. We rushed over so we could see it through the gate. Trains go all the way up to Albany and Maine on the tracks. I like to watch them go by. It's one of the few places you can see the trains up close.

"Hey, did you ever put a penny on a train track?" Zeke asked me as we peered through the gate.

"No, why would I do that?" I replied.

"If you put a penny on the track and a train runs over it, the penny gets flattened, like a pancake," he said. "It's cool."

"Couldn't that derail the train?" I asked.

"A penny derail a train?" Zeke said with a snort. "You nuts?"

"Did *you* ever do that?" I asked him. "Put a penny on a train track?"

"No, but I heard kids talk about doing it."

"Sounds like one of those urban legends," I told him. "I bet the penny just gets knocked off the track."

"No, I'm pretty sure it's for real," he replied.

The train tracks were just a few feet away, on the other side of the gate. You can't climb over the gate because it goes all the way up to the top of the arch. There was no lock on the gate, but it looked like it was all rusted shut. Just for the heck of it, I gave it a yank.

It swung open with a loud creaking sound.

Zeke and I looked at each other and smiled.

"You wanna do it?" we both said at the same time.

"I will if you will," he said. "You got any change on you?"

I reached into my pocket. I had a quarter, a nickel, and four pennies.

I peered inside the dark tunnel. There were signs on the wall: KEEP OFF THE TRACKS. NO TRES-PASSING. NEW YORK CITY POLICE DEPARTMENT.

"This is illegal, you know," I pointed out.

"So is jaywalking," said Zeke.

"What if we get caught?" I asked.

"We won't get caught."

We tiptoed into the tunnel and closed the heavy gate behind us. It was mostly dark in there, with a little light shining down through a grate in the ceiling. We could see graffiti written on the walls and some rubble scat-tered around the ground. Something smelled bad. The gravel crunched under our feet.

"There are probably rats in here," I said, almost whispering.

"I don't want to know what I'm smelling,"

Zeke said, his voice echoing off the walls of the tunnel.

"How often do the trains come?" I asked.

"All the time," Zeke replied. "My dad takes it to Albany to go to work. They come every half hour or so."

"We really shouldn't be doing this," I said. "You hear stories about kids getting killed doing dumb stuff like this."

"Dumb kids get killed," Zeke told me. "We're not dumb."

Let me say right here that putting pennies on train tracks is definitely one of those things you *shouldn't* try at home. It's just stupid and dangerous. But my mom once told me that the human brain isn't fully formed until we're in our twenties, and that's why kids can't be thrown in jail for doing the stupid things we sometimes do.

Zeke got down on his hands and knees and put his ear against the track.

"What are you doing?" I asked him. "You wanna get your head crushed?"

"They say that if you put your ear against

the steel track, you can feel the vibrations of a train coming from miles away," he told me.

"That's probably another one of those urban legends."

"No, it's true," Zeke insisted. "Hey, I think I feel something! A train is coming! Quick, put the coins on the track!"

I looked around to see if anybody was watching before digging the coins out of my pocket again and carefully laying them in a row on the track. I could hear the rumbling of the train now, and I could see two headlights in the distance.

"I see it!" I said. "This is gonna be cool."

Zeke scampered out of the way. I was about to do the same when I felt a tug on my left foot.

"Wait up!" I shouted. "I think my shoelace is stuck!"

"Very funny," Zeke replied.

"I *mean* it!" I shouted. "The tip is stuck under the rail!"

"Well pull it out!" Zeke yelled at me.

I tried to pull it out.

"I can't!" I shouted back. "I can't see it! It's too dark in here!"

Now we could both see the light of the train approaching in the distance. This was not funny. This was dead serious. My shoelace was somehow stuck under the rail. The thought crossed my mind—*I could die in this tunnel*. I fumbled with the lace trying to get it loose.

"The engineer will stop the train if he has to!" Zeke shouted as he waved his hands in the air. "He must be able to see us by now."

But the train was not slowing down. Nobody was putting on the brakes. Why would they? The engineer probably wasn't even looking ahead. There was no reason to think anybody would be inside the tunnel.

The rumble had become a thunderous roar that echoed off the walls as the train got closer. I kept tugging at my shoelace, desperately trying to get it loose. Sweat was pouring down my forehead. I wiped it away with my sleeve.

"Hurry up!" shouted Zeke.

I looked up. The train was closer.

I felt my heart racing. In a few seconds the train would be right on top of me.

"Forget about the lace!" shouted Zeke. "Just pull your sneaker off!"

"I can't!" I shouted back. "The knot is too tight!"

Zeke crawled over to try to pull my sneaker off. But he couldn't get it off either.

"Yank it!"

"I'm trying!"

There was no more time. The train was right on top of us. There was nothing we could do.

"Roll!" Zeke shouted, as he dove out of the way.

I rolled my whole body over, stretching out so I was as far away from the rail as possible. My shoelace was taut, still attached. If I was going to lose my foot, that was the price I'd pay for my stupidity. I just didn't want to lose my life.

The train sounded like a rocket taking off. I couldn't communicate with Zeke anymore. The noise was too loud. I covered my ears to block it out.

As the train roared past, it must have sliced through my shoelace, because I fell backward, landing on the rocks next to the tracks and hitting the ground hard.

And that's all I remember.

THE BOX

I think I was dreaming. It was something about a test at school that I didn't study for.

Then I woke up, and I sensed immediately that something was wrong. I felt lousy. I had a headache. My nose and throat were sore. But it was more than that. Something was different. My bed didn't feel right. My pillow didn't feel right. I felt sore all over. It was like I had run a marathon or something. But I didn't remember doing anything different before I went to sleep. I didn't remember going to Riverside Park with Zeke, or anything about the train tracks. Not then. Not yet.

Somebody was holding my right hand. That was strange.

I was hesitant to open my eyes. They didn't want to open. It was like they had forgotten how to blink. I had to force them open.

The first thing I heard when I opened my eyes was the sound of my mother screaming.

"You're awake!" she shrieked. "He's awake! Harry's awake! My baby is awake!"

The next thing I knew, she was all over me, hugging and kissing me and crying tears of joy.

"Harry's back!" she shouted. "Nurse! Nurse!"

"Can you close the shades?" I mumbled, shielding my eyes.

Everything seemed so *bright*. My eyes had been shut for so long, it seemed. They needed to adjust to the light. My voice felt rough. My mother was hollering like she had won the lottery or something.

I looked around. I was in a hospital room. There were a bunch of machines beeping, like those old-time video games. Tubes were going into my nose, and an IV was in my arm. I had never even spent a night in a hospital before. I wasn't even *born* in a hospital. So I didn't know if all this stuff was normal or not.

A couple of nurses rushed in, one of them a woman and the other a man. They seemed really happy to see me.

I looked myself over, searching for clues about what had happened to me. I had all my limbs. There was no blood. No cast. I could move all my fingers. It didn't seem like I had any broken bones or anything. I couldn't imagine why I was in the hospital, or why everybody was acting like it was such a big deal. All I did was wake up.

"Where am I?" I asked. My mother was too emotional to answer.

"Mount Sinai Hospital," the male nurse told me. "You're in the ICU. We're going to check your vital signs. Then the doctor will come in to look at you."

ICU? That's the Intensive Care Unit. That's where they put people who need...intensive care, I guess. But I didn't even know what that meant. I thought *everybody* in a hospital is supposed to get intensive care. That's why they're in a hospital.

"Why am I here?" I asked.

"You were in a coma, honey," said the female nurse. Then she told her partner, "Vital signs look good."

A *coma*? That's *serious* stuff. Being in a coma is like being somewhere between sleep and death, but probably closer to death. I don't know much about it, but I do know that some people who are in a coma *never* come out of it.

"How long was I out?" I asked.

"A week," my mother said, wiping her eyes with a handful of tissues. "I didn't think you'd ever wake up."

"Your mom was here the whole time," the female nurse said. "She's a real hero."

A *week*? No wonder I was sore all over. I needed to move. I started to roll over so I could put my feet on the floor and stand up.

"Not so fast, cowboy," the male nurse said, pushing me back down on the bed.

I wasn't strong enough to resist.

"What happened to me?" I asked.

"You were playing by the railroad tracks at Riverside Park," my mother explained, still sniffling a little. "You must have hit your head on something. You had a concussion. Honey, I'm so glad you're back!" And then she started crying again.

Railroad tracks? I had no memory of being around the railroad tracks. My mom didn't seem mad that I had done such a stupid thing. She just looked so grateful that I was alive.

The nurses were checking my vital signs—whatever they are—when another lady came in. Her nametag said "Dr. Fischer" on it.

"Well, it's about *time* you woke up!" she said, winking at me. "I thought we might have to start charging your mother rent to stay here. She *never* goes home."

The doctor put her hand on the back of my head and moved it around.

"The swelling has gone down significantly,"

she said. "That's a good sign. You don't have a subdural hematoma."

"That sounds scary," I said.

"It is," the doctor replied. "How do you feel?"

"Weak," I told her.

"That's normal," she explained. "You haven't moved your muscles in seven days."

The doctor shined a little flashlight in my eyes and asked me a bunch of questions any dope could answer: "What year is it?" "Who is the president of the United States?" "How old are you?" That sort of thing. I answered all of them, no problem. Then she told me a little bit about concussions.

Apparently, a concussion means "a stunning, damaging, or shattering effect from a hard blow to the head." Football players get them all the time, and it's a big controversy over whether kids should be allowed to play football.

"Are you hungry, Harry?" the doctor asked.

"No." And then I asked, "If I haven't eaten anything for a week, how come I'm not hungry?"

"We've been giving you nutrition through the tube in your nose," the doctor told me.

Eating through my nose? Gross.

"What kind of nutrition?" I asked.

"A fluid with a balance of protein, carbohydrate, fats, sugars, vitamins..."

"It sounds disgusting."

"You're going to be just fine," Dr. Fischer said, writing something on a clipboard.

"So can I go home?" I asked.

"I want you to stay here one more night, just so we can keep an eye on you," she said. "You may have a little difficulty standing and walking at first. The physical therapist will talk to you about that. When you get home, I want you to take it easy for a few weeks. No sports. No parties. And let's stay away from railroad tracks, shall we?"

"Okay."

"Any questions for me?" the doctor said.

"Am I going to be normal again?" I asked.

"Were you ever normal?" she replied.

When I didn't laugh at her little joke, she said, "Young people usually bounce back quickly from these things. I think you'll be just fine. If you continue to have a headache, or nausea or vomiting, we'll take another look."

When Dr. Fischer left, I noticed for the first time that the windowsill was filled with flowers, boxes of candy, cards, and letters. I struggled to prop myself up in the bed. My arms felt so weak. My mother put a pillow behind me, and pushed some button on a remote control that made the top of the bed rise up a little. Then she handed me a few of the get-well cards. They were written by my classmates at school. Really nice notes. Even a few of the kids I didn't particularly like said they missed me and hoped I'd get better soon.

Mom and I were looking at the cards when there was a knock at the door. It was Zeke.

"Remember me?" he asked cautiously, as if he really thought I might not remember him. I gave him a fist bump.

"Zeke saved your life," my mother told me. "If he hadn't been around to run and get help, I don't know that you'd be with us today, Harry."

I looked at Zeke. He locked eyes with me and silently shook his head very slightly to let me know my mother didn't know the whole story.

"You look good, you lazy bum," he told me. "I wish *I* could go to sleep for a week."

"What about school?" I asked Zeke. "I must have missed a ton of homework."

"Don't worry about that stuff now," he replied. "You'll catch up. The important thing is that you came out of it and you're gonna get better."

My mom got up and told me to smile so she could take a picture of me with her phone. Then she took her purse.

"I'm going to go out in the hall to make some phone calls and tell everybody the good news," she said. "I'm sure you boys have a lot to talk about."

As soon as my mom left, I turned to Zeke.

"Okay, what happened?" I whispered. "What were we doing by the railroad tracks?"

"You don't remember?" he asked.

"I remember going to the park," I told him. "After that, it's a blur."

Zeke reached into his pocket and pulled out a small, flat piece of silver metal. He handed it to me. It was shiny.

"What's that?" I asked.

"It *used* to be a quarter," Zeke told me. "Now it's a flattened piece of whatever they make quarters out of."

I was beginning to remember. "We put this on the train tracks?" I asked, handing it back to him.

"Yeah."

"Why?" I asked.

"Because we're idiots," Zeke told me. "It was a stupid thing to do. Just as the train was coming, your shoelace got caught in the track. You couldn't get it loose. At the last second, you rolled out of the way. That's when you hit your head. It was all my fault. I'm really sorry, man. I'm so glad you're okay. I don't know what I would have done if you didn't come out of it."

Zeke looked like he was getting choked up. I opened one of the boxes of candy somebody sent me and gave him a piece. That seemed to cheer him up a little. He told me that after the train passed by and I was unconscious, he dragged me out of the tunnel and ran to get help. He wasn't sure if I was dead or alive.

When my mom came back to the room, she took more pictures of me and hugged me a lot. One of the nurses suggested she go home and get a good night's sleep. Mom didn't want to at first, but when I assured her that I was okay, she finally agreed to leave. She offered to give Zeke a taxi ride home.

"I'll be back in the morning," she said, kissing me on my forehead. "I'm so glad you're with us, honey."

I was by myself. I turned on the TV with the remote at my side and flipped through the channels, but nothing good was on. I skimmed a few of the cards and letters people had sent, but I was too tired to go through them. Why was I so tired if I had just been asleep for a week?

There were a bunch of boxes of candy on the windowsill next to the bed. I reached over and picked up one of them. There was a ribbon wrapped around it. I knew I wasn't supposed to eat anything until I spoke with the speech therapist, but what harm could one piece of candy do?

I untied the ribbon and ripped the wrapping paper off the box. There was no note attached to it. I opened the box and was surprised to find that there was no candy inside.

Instead, there was a cell phone. It was one of those old flip phones people used before everybody had smartphones.

I wondered—why would somebody give me a cell phone? All my friends know that my mom won't let me have one. They make fun of me about that all the time. And if they saw me using a flip phone, they'd make fun of me for *that*. The only reason I even *know* about flip phones is because I've seen them on old TV shows.

One of the nurses came in to check on me. I slipped the phone under my pillow. I didn't want anybody to see it, and possibly let my mom know about it.

The nurse looked at one of the beeping screens and said she was monitoring my blood oxygen level. She wrote something down, and left the room.

I reached under my pillow and pulled out the flip phone. Maybe it was a gag gift, I figured. The thing was so old. It couldn't possibly still work.

I flipped it open anyway and pushed the power button.

The screen lit up.

YOU COULD HAVE ESCAPED

I couldn't believe it. That phone must have been ten years old, at least. It had a black-and-white screen! And the battery hadn't died? Amazing. The screen doesn't light up unless the phone works, right? That's what I always thought. Not that I know much about cell phones. But technology moves so fast. I just assume anything that's so old isn't going to work anymore.

Of course, I tried to test the phone right

away. I needed a phone number to call. There's this horribly annoying TV commercial for a company that asks people to donate their cars to raise money for underprivileged kids. I've heard their commercial about a million times, and the 800 number would be stuck in my head forever. I dialed it, and waited.

Nothing. Nobody picked up. There was no recording. The phone didn't even ring.

I tried calling Zeke's cell phone number, which I had also memorized because I've called it so many times from our landline at home. Nothing.

I tried dialing a few other random phone numbers. The same thing happened. The screen lit up, but the flip phone couldn't make an outgoing call. Too bad. Just when I was getting my hopes up.

But that made sense, I guess. You have to pay extra money to get cell phone service, I think. My mom pays over a hundred dollars a month. She's always complaining about it, because she doesn't use her cell phone very much. And I know she would never agree to pay for service for my phone too. Bummer. I put the phone back in the box and went to sleep.

When I woke up the next morning, my mom was already in the hospital room with me. My headache was gone. The nurses were monitoring me closely, but it wasn't necessary. I was feeling just fine. They took the tubes out of me. The physical therapist, a really nice lady, helped me get out of bed and walk up and down the hall. I had no problems. She showed me some exercises to strengthen my muscles. Then the speech therapist came in and did something called a "swallow test" on me. I must have passed the test, because after that I was given real food—eggs, home fries, and toast with jam. It tasted great.

Dr. Fischer came in, looked at my chart, and gave me the okay to be discharged from the hospital. My mom was overjoyed. When she wasn't looking, I stashed the box with the flip phone in my backpack. Someday, I hoped, I might be able to make it work.

I told my mother that I didn't want to bring home all the flowers that people had sent, and she arranged for them to be given to other patients in the hospital who didn't have a family. But I boxed up the candy to bring home with me. I'm no dummy! I said goodbye to all the nurses and doctors who had taken care of me and been so nice while I was in the hospital.

My mom had to sign a bunch of paperwork to get me discharged. Then an orderly rolled a wheelchair into my room to bring me downstairs.

"I really don't need this," I told him. "I can walk fine."

"Hospital rules," he replied.

I said that was awfully nice, but my mom whispered in my ear that the hospital wasn't just being nice to me. If a patient falls or gets hurt on the way out of the building, they might sue. So even if you only have a hangnail, they put you in a wheelchair until you're out of the hospital. Down on the street, my mom hailed a taxi.

• • •

It felt good to be home. The first thing I did when I got to my room was take the phone out of my backpack and stash it in the back of the junk drawer in my night table. I stuck it under some stuff so my mom wouldn't come across it while cleaning.

For the first couple of days I was home, my mom treated me like a fragile flower. She didn't want me to lift a finger. But soon life returned to normal. I went back to school and everybody was really happy to see me. On Thursday, my mom didn't want me to go to Zeke's birthday party, but I talked her into letting me go.

Have you ever been to an escape-room party? They're actually cooler than I thought. Basically, you get locked in a room and you have an hour to figure out how to get out. There's usually some kind of a theme to the room, like it's a haunted house, a space station, or a secret laboratory. You have to solve a series of riddles and clues that lead to a solution in order to escape. Escape rooms were a big thing a few years ago. Everybody was doing them.

So Zeke and I, his dad, and a couple of Zeke's other friends from his church went to this escape room place in Harlem. They have four different rooms. One is called "The Hoosegow." One is called "Zombie Attack." One is called "Treasure of the Catacombs." The room we were locked in was called "The Dungeon." It was described as "a human research project."

The room looked like a prison cell and everything in the room was there for a reason. Everything was a clue. For instance, there were a bunch of gummy bears glued to one wall. At first we just thought that was strange, but then we figured out that the numbers of red, green, yellow, and blue gummy bears gave us the solution to a four-digit combination lock—4-5-2-3.

The lock opened a cabinet. There was only one thing inside the cabinet—a flashlight. But it wasn't a regular flashlight. It was a black-light flashlight. When we turned off the lights and shined the flashlight at the wall, a bunch of letters appeared there that couldn't be seen in the regular light. That letter code opened up another lock.

You had to solve a bunch of puzzles like that in a specific order to get out of the room. There was a timer on the wall that counted down to tell us how much time we had left.

I won't bore you with all the details. The words we saw on the wall didn't make any sense, but we noticed that the first letter of each one spelled "skoob." That's where we got stuck.

The puzzles were really hard. When the timer clicked down to ten minutes and we still had a few clues to solve, we knew we weren't going to get out of the room. We were stumped.

The whole thing was exhausting for me, because there was no place to sit and I hadn't done a lot of standing in a long time. It was still fun anyway. When the timer buzzed, the door opened and one of the employees came in to "rescue" us.

"What does the word *skoob* mean?" I asked her.

"Sorry, but I'm not allowed tell you the answers to the clues," she replied. "Come back and try again sometime."

"Oh, come on!"

She told us not to feel bad, because most people don't figure out how to escape from the room. She gave us discount coupons for a return visit.

Afterward, Zeke's parents took us all out for dinner at this place that makes amazing ice-cream sundaes.

It had been a long day for me, and I fell into bed early. I tried to read a little bit from my science book for school, but felt my eyelids closing. So I turned off my light and pulled my covers up around me. That's when I heard a soft buzzing sound.

Bzzzzz...bzzzzz...bzzzzz...

What's *that?* It sounded very close, like it was in my room. I flipped the light back on and looked around. The buzzing sound seemed to be coming from my night table.

I opened the drawer.

The cell phone I had stashed in there was vibrating!

I flipped it open.

These words were on the screen...

"YOU COULD HAVE ESCAPED."

That was it. Huh! *The phone actually works,* I thought to myself. But I figured it had to be a prank.

"Who is this?" I whispered. I didn't want my mom to hear me from her bedroom. "Zeke?"

There was no response.

Of course not, I thought, slapping myself in the forehead. It was a *text,* not a call. The phone didn't work as a *phone,* but it could transmit texts. Or it could receive them, anyway.

"Who is this?" I tapped clumsily on the little keypad, making a few typos along the way and correcting them.

There was no response.

"Is this you, Zeke?" I tapped.

Nothing.

It was probably the escape room place, I figured. They were taunting me. I'll bet they send that text out to *everybody* who doesn't escape so they'll come back and try again. Zeke must have gotten the same message. I made a mental note to ask him about it at school the next day.

I put the flip phone back in the drawer and lay there with my hands behind my head. It was hard to sleep because I couldn't stop thinking. How did anybody get that number to send the text? And why would they be sending a text to this random phone in the first place? I never gave them a number. I didn't even know the number myself.

These thoughts were going around and around in my brain. And one more: Who left the box with a flip phone in my hospital room? And why?

For a moment, I considered getting up and going to tell my mom what was going on. But then I thought the better of it. If she knew I had a phone and that it worked, even just to receive texts, she'd probably take it away from me.

I rolled over and was almost asleep when...

Bzzzzz... bzzzzz... bzzzzz...

I turned on the light, opened the drawer, and took out the cell phone again.

"YOU SHOULD HAVE ESCAPED."

It *had* to be Zeke, messing with me. He must have been the one who sent the old cell phone to my hospital room, as a joke. That guy cracks me up.

"How could I have escaped?" I tapped.

A few seconds passed, and then this appeared on the screen....

"SKOOB IS BOOKS BACKWARD. THERE WAS A BOOKSHELF ON THE WALL."

"So?" I tapped.

"ONE OF THE BOOKS HAD A KEY INSIDE. IT WOULD HAVE OPENED THE DESK DRAWER."

Of *course*! It was so simple! They probably cut out the center of the book's pages to hide the key. We should have been able to figure that out when we were in the escape room. The solution was right under our noses. Zeke must have been thinking about it all night.

"How do you know that?" I tapped.

A few more seconds passed, and then this appeared on the screen....

"LET'S JUST SAY I'M GOOD AT ESCAP-
ING FROM THINGS."

"Pretty smart, Zeke," I tapped.

"IT'S NOT ZEKE," my screen said.

"Then who are you?" I tapped.

Three dots appeared on the screen, and they were there for a long time, which suggested that he—or she—was writing a long reply. Finally the dots disappeared. I was a little more than surprised when they were replaced by just one word:

"HOUDINI."

THE GREAT MYSTERY

Okay, now I was *sure* I was being pranked.

Zeke is always pulling crazy stuff like this. He likes to mess with people, especially me. He'll put toothpaste in your Oreos or cotton balls in your sneakers just for laughs. One time he told me the next day was going to be "Pajama Day" and everybody was going to wear pajamas to school. So I wore my pajamas. But when I got to school, I was the only kid wearing pajamas! I don't know if I'll ever forgive Zeke for that one.

It was like putting the coins on the train tracks. Zeke likes to do weird stuff that most other people wouldn't think of doing. Not bad stuff, mind you. He doesn't break the law or intentionally hurt anybody. He just likes to do weird stuff. That's the way his brain works, I guess.

I was staring at the word "HOUDINI" on the phone screen when it was replaced by another text....

"THE ESCAPE ROOM WAS A PIECE OF CAKE. ANYBODY SHOULD HAVE BEEN ABLE TO GET OUT."

"Knock it off, Zeke," I tapped on the phone. "It's not funny."

"I AM NOT ZEKE," appeared on my screen after a few seconds. "I AM HARRY HOUDINI."

I knew that was a lie. Harry Houdini died way back in 1926. Zeke didn't know the story of how it happened, but I did. I had read all about it.

If you've ever heard anybody say that

Houdini died from a punch in the stomach, it's basically true. Here's what happened:

Houdini was doing a bunch of shows in the fall of 1926. During a show in Albany, New York, he was about to perform his famous Water Torture Cell trick when a wire twisted and he fractured his left ankle. Houdini took pride in not giving in to pain, so the show went on. (In fact, when he wanted to prove how tough he was, Houdini would sometimes stick a needle through his cheek.)

Despite the broken ankle, he struggled through two shows in Albany, then did a show in Schenectady, and after that it was on to Montreal, limping the whole time.

On October 22, during the afternoon before his show, Houdini gave a talk at McGill University. During the talk, one of the students drew a sketch of him. Houdini was impressed, and invited the student to come to the theater where he was performing the next day to draw another one for his collection.

While Houdini was lying down on a couch posing for his picture, another student knocked on the dressing-room door. His name was J. Gordon Whitehead. They talked about various subjects, and then Whitehead suddenly asked, "Is it true, Mr. Houdini, that you can resist the hardest blows struck to the abdomen?"

Houdini played along, letting Whitehead feel the muscles in his arms.

"Would you mind if I delivered a few blows to your abdomen, Mr. Houdini?" Whitehead asked.

Houdini said it was okay. He was lying on a couch, remember, because of his broken ankle. Suddenly, without giving Houdini a chance to tense up his muscles and get ready, Whitehead punched him four or five times in the stomach. Whitehead was a big man, and he hit Houdini as hard as he could.

Houdini took the blows, but was in serious pain afterward. At his show the next night, he was sweating and had to lie down during intermission. After the show, he couldn't dress himself. He was in too much pain.

Detroit was the next stop on the tour. When he arrived, Houdini had a temperature of

102 degrees. A doctor was called, and he said that Houdini had acute appendicitis. Houdini insisted on doing his show anyway, although his temperature was now at 104. He struggled through the performance, and collapsed at the end.

He was taken to the hospital and rushed into surgery. Doctors removed his appendix, which had ruptured. He felt a little better, but then Houdini took a turn for the worse. Poison from his appendix had seeped into his intestines. Another operation had to be performed.

It didn't work. Houdini died that Sunday—Halloween—at Grace Hospital in Detroit. His last words were "I can't fight anymore." He was just fifty-two years old.

"Houdini is dead," I tapped on the little keypad.

The reply came quickly. It was just two letters....

"SO?"

I thought that was all, but then a torrent of words scrolled up my little screen....

"WHEN WE DIE, ONLY OUR PHYSICAL BODY DIES. THE SPIRIT SURVIVES."

What?!

"DEATH IS NOT THE END OF LIFE. IT IS JUST A CHANGE IN LIFE. LIKE A CATER-PILLAR TURNING INTO A BUTTERFLY."

Wow. This was a pretty elaborate prank somebody was pulling on me. Whoever was behind it had put some thought and effort into it.

"So you're claiming," I tapped, "that the dead can communicate with the living. And you're dead?"

"CORRECT," was the reply. "WE EXIST IN PARALLEL WORLDS."

Oh yeah, spiritualism—the belief that the dead can communicate with the living. All the books I've read about Houdini talk about spiritualism. It was an up-and-coming religion in Houdini's day. Spiritualists believed that the world was made of two substances, matter and spirit. We can see and feel matter, but spirit is invisible. It can't be perceived through our senses.

It all began in 1848 with three sisters named Fox. They claimed to hear mysterious knocking noises made by spirits who haunted their home in Hydesville, New York. Word got around, and soon the Fox sisters were celebrities, giving demonstrations before big crowds and making lots of money. They confessed they were faking it all in 1888, but by then hundreds of spiritualists had popped up all over the country, claiming to be able to reunite grieving people with their dead relatives.

Spiritualism was really popular around 1920, after so many soldiers had been killed in World War I and millions of people had died in a flu epidemic. In Houdini's day, it was the phony mediums and fortune-tellers who served as "voices from the spirit world." Now it looked like those same kinds of fakers were doing it with cell phones. The more things change, the more they stay the same.

The thing is, Houdini *hated* spiritualism. He saw how fake mediums—using tricks just like those used by magicians—would take money from grief-stricken people. He actually spent the last few years of his life trying to expose fraudulent spiritualists.

"You can't be Houdini," I tapped. "He didn't believe in spiritualism."

"LET'S JUST SAY THAT BEING DEAD HAS A WAY OF CHANGING ONE'S MIND."

I will admit one thing. If *anybody* could come back from the grave and communicate with the living, it would be Harry Houdini. He said so himself before he died. He used to make arrangements with his friends saying that whichever one of them "punctured the veil of death" first would try to contact the other. Houdini called it "the great mystery."

"I AM ON THE OTHER SIDE NOW," it said on my screen.

Look, I'm no dummy. There are a lot of scammers out there, and I wasn't going to fall for this one. It was only a matter of time before this "Houdini" character—whoever he was—would ask me to send money. Scam artists are always trying to rip you off.

"I don't believe you," I tapped.

There was a long pause. I thought I had

heard the last of him. He would just hang up and move on to the next number on his list, hoping to find a sucker. But then another torrent of words scrolled up my screen....

"I WAS BORN ON MARCH 24TH, 1874. IN BUDAPEST, HUNGARY. ONE OF SEVEN BROTHERS & SISTERS. CAME TO U.S. AND SETTLED IN WISCONSIN. I RAN AWAY FROM HOME AT 12. MARRIED BESS RAYMOND. STARTED DOING HANDCUFF ESCAPES IN 1895."

The phantom texter was rattling off Houdini's biography, as if I didn't already know it. He said he was known as "The King of Handcuffs" by 1899, and a couple of years later he had become one of the most famous men in the world. He claimed to have escaped from drowning two thousand times. He got out of 12,500 straitjackets and opened 8,300 padlocks. Along the way, he singlehandedly created an entire form of entertainment—the escape artist.

"WHAT MORE CAN I TELL YOU?" he texted. "I AM HOUDINI!"

I still wasn't impressed.

"You could have learned all that stuff from Wikipedia," I tapped.

"WIKI WHAT?" came back. "IF YOU DON'T BELIEVE ME, ASK ME SOMETHING THAT ONLY THE REAL HARRY HOUDINI WOULD KNOW."

Hmmmm. Well, he asked for it. I know a *lot* about Houdini.

"What did you have in your hand your whole life?" I tapped.

"A BULLET," he texted back right away. "I GOT INTO AN ARGUMENT WITH SOME GAMBLERS WHEN I WAS A YOUNG MAN, AND ONE OF THEM SHOT ME. THE DOCTORS COULDN'T REMOVE THE BULLET."

That was an easy one. I tried to think of something that hardly anybody knows about Houdini.

"After the Wright Brothers invented the airplane, you became a pilot," I tapped. "What was your biggest accomplishment in that area?

"I WAS THE FIRST PERSON TO FLY A PLANE IN AUSTRALIA," he texted back.

Wow, that was right! But I still wasn't convinced. Far from it. Anybody could claim to be anybody in a text. That's why we're told to be careful when we communicate with people online. Zeke didn't know all that stuff about Houdini. So it couldn't be him. But maybe it was some Houdini expert who was pranking me. Maybe it was one of those guys who wrote a book about Houdini. We had a whole shelf of them in the living room downstairs.

Or maybe it was some magician who is obsessed with Houdini. Magicians are in the business of deception. Their job is to mislead people. Maybe he's misleading me. I wasn't going to fall for it. It could be anybody.

"Those questions are all easily Googleable," I tapped.

"GOOGLEABLE?"

Oh sure, it made perfect sense for him to pretend he never heard of Google. The real Houdini wouldn't know anything about stuff that took place after 1926.

Then it hit me. I would ask him about something that's not on Google. Information that isn't available *anywhere*. I would ask him the secrets of his magic.

"How did you do the East Indian Needle Trick?" I tapped.

The East Indian Needle Trick was one of Houdini's strangest and most amazing stunts. He would take a hundred needles and put them in his mouth. Then he would put twenty yards of thread in his mouth. Then he would drink from a glass of water to "swallow" it all. A few seconds later, he would reach into his mouth and pull out the thread—with the needles attached to it, each needle a few inches apart!

It was simply amazing. And Houdini did a similar trick using razor blades. I always wondered how he did it.

It didn't take long for a reply to come back: "I HID A THREADED SET OF NEEDLES BETWEEN MY UPPER GUM AND CHEEKS THE WHOLE TIME," he explained. "AFTER I PULLED IT OUT OF MY MOUTH, I WOULD GET RID OF THE OTHER NEEDLES IN THE GLASS OF WATER AND MY ASSISTANT WOULD TAKE IT AWAY."

Of course! I should have been able to figure that out.

"What about walking through walls?" I tapped. "How did you do that?"

It was another Houdini classic. A team of bricklayers would come up on stage and actually build a brick wall while the audience watched. Houdini would be on one side of the wall. Then a curtain would be placed in front, and Houdini would magically appear on the other side of the wall.

"THERE WAS A TRAP DOOR IN THE MIDDLE OF THE STAGE," came the reply. "WHEN IT WAS OPENED, THE CARPET SAGGED JUST ENOUGH FOR ME TO SQUEEZE UNDER THE WALL AND COME UP ON THE OTHER SIDE."

Wow. Whoever this guy really was, he sure knew his stuff.

"What about the trunk escape?" I tapped. "How did you pull *that* off?"

The trunk escape was one of Houdini's most famous tricks. That's the one in which he would be locked up in chains and put inside a large trunk. The trunk would be nailed shut with dozens of nails, and then dropped into a river. People would line the banks, freaking out while it seemed like Houdini was drowning. A minute or two later, he would bob to the surface, smiling and free of the chains.

"SIMPLE," was the reply. "THE TRUNK HAD A HIDDEN PANEL HELD ON BY TWO SHORT NAILS. I WOULD GET OUT OF THE CHAINS WHILE THE TRUNK WAS NAILED SHUT AND THEN PUSH OUT THE TRICK PANEL UNDERWATER."

"Yeah, but how did you get out of the handcuffs and chains when you were locked in the trunk?" I tapped.

"THERE ARE A MILLION WAYS," he texted back. "IF YOU HIT MOST HANDCUFFS ON A HARD SERVICE, THEY WILL OPEN. IF THAT DIDN'T WORK, I WOULD PICK THE LOCK WITH A SHOESTRING, HAIRPIN, PAPER CLIP, OR PIANO WIRE."

I knew very well that before an escape, Houdini would invite people to come up on stage to look him over carefully to make sure he wasn't hiding anything he might use to pick a lock. Sometimes they even had a doctor examine him.

"Where did you hide all that lock-picking stuff?" I asked.

"SOMETIMES BESS WOULD SLIP ME SOMETHING WHILE SHE WAS GIVING ME A KISS," was the reply. SOMETIMES I HID IT IN A FAKE HOLLOW FINGER. THEY NEVER COUNT YOUR FINGERS."

Wow. This guy was blowing my mind. He was either really good, or he was really Houdini.

But he *couldn't* be Houdini! Houdini was long dead. And you can't communicate with dead people—who, by the way, didn't have cell phones in 1926. I had to keep telling myself not to let this guy make a fool out of me.

"Knowing all that stuff only *proves* you're a fake!" I tapped. "Everybody knows that magicians never reveal their secrets."

"DEAD ONES WOULD," was the response. "WHAT DO I HAVE TO LOSE? MY LIFE IS OVER."

He had a point, I suppose. If he was really dead, there was no reason to hold onto his secrets anymore. He might as well tell the world. My head was spinning.

"ARE YOU CONVINCED *NOW*?" it said on my screen.

I thought about it for a long time before replying.

"No," I tapped. But honestly, I wasn't so sure anymore. Maybe the guy really *was* Houdini, talking to me from the grave.

"IF I COULD NOT EXPLAIN MY TRICKS, YOU WOULD HAVE SAID I WASN'T HOUDINI. AND WHEN I EXPLAINED MY TRICKS, YOU SAID I WASN'T HOUDINI. WHAT DO I HAVE TO DO TO PROVE I AM WHO I SAY I AM?"

"I don't know," I admitted.

"YOU HAVE ASKED ENOUGH QUESTIONS. NOW LET ME ASK A QUESTION OF YOU."

"Go ahead," I tapped. I can play along.

"WHO ARE YOU?"

"You don't know who I am?" I tapped.

"NO."

"My name is Harry Mancini," I tapped. "I'm eleven years old."

"AND WHAT YEAR IS IT?"

"It is the 21st century," I tapped, tapping out the year to be more specific. There was a long pause.

"NOW IT IS YOU WHO IS MAKING THINGS UP."

"I swear it's true," I tapped.

"WHERE DO YOU LIVE?"

"New York City," I tapped.

"WHERE IN NYC?"

"In Harlem," I tapped.

"WHERE IN HARLEM?"

"278 West 113th Street," I tapped before it occurred to me that I shouldn't give out my address to a total stranger.

"THAT'S MY HOUSE!" he replied.

"I know!" I tapped.

"YOU LIVE IN MY HOUSE?"

Something occurred to me.

"How come you could tell me exactly how I could have gotten out of the escape room," I tapped, "but you didn't know where or when I live?"

I waited for a response. Nothing.

Aha! I had him! He couldn't answer that. He was a fake! I don't know how he pulled it off, but he did it.

"Why did you contact…" I couldn't tap in the word "me." It didn't show up on the screen.

Then I noticed that the screen was blank.

The battery of the cell phone had died.

A PIECE OF JUNK

The next day I got to school early. I needed to speak to Zeke before first period.

"I gotta talk to you," I said when I saw him at his locker.

"I gotta talk to you too, Harry," he told me. "You won't believe what happened to me last night. Five minutes after I went to bed there was a siren outside my window. I figured it was an ambulance or a fire engine or something, so I got out of bed to see what was going on. And do you know what was out there?"

"What?" I asked.

"It was some kid with a boom box playing a rap song with a siren sound in the middle of it."

"That's it?" I asked. "*That's* the exciting thing that happened to you last night?"

"Yeah. I thought it was pretty cool."

I looked into his eyes to see if he was putting me on. With Zeke, you could never tell.

"What did you want to talk to *me* about?" he asked.

"You really don't know, do you?"

"No," he replied. "How could I possibly know?"

"So you didn't do it, did you?"

"No," he said. "Well, that depends. Do *what*?"

I told him about the cell phone and my text conversation with "Harry Houdini." He couldn't believe it either.

"Your story was way better than mine," he admitted when I finished.

"The guy was *really* convincing," I said. "He knew everything about Houdini. He even knew that Houdini had a bullet stuck in his hand most of his life. Hardly *anybody* knows that."

"So who was it?" Zeke asked.

"I don't know!" I told him. "I thought it was you."

"I swear it wasn't me," Zeke said. "And how do you even know it was a guy? It could have been a woman. It could have been a kid. It could have been a bot. With text, it could have been *anybody*."

"You're right," I agreed. "I have no idea who it was. Do you think it could really have been Houdini?"

"I don't believe in ghosts or supernatural stuff like that," Zeke said.

"Me neither," I replied. "But you never know. Weird stuff happens."

"Did he try to sell you anything?" Zeke asked. "Did he ask you for money or your Social Security number? That would be a sure sign it was a scam."

"That's the thing," I told Zeke. "He didn't ask for a dime. It was like he just wanted to talk to somebody."

"I'll say this much," Zeke told me. "That was a great prank. I wish I had come up with that idea. But let me ask you this. No offense, Harry, but are you sure you're not still messed up in the head a little bit after being in a coma?"

"I'm fine, Zeke," I told him.

"I mean, maybe you were dreaming, or hallucinating, or something."

"I wasn't dreaming," I insisted. "I wasn't hallucinating. It *happened*."

"Then somebody was messing with you," Zeke said. "Lemme see the cell phone."

I was about to get the phone out of my backpack when the bell rang for first period. I had to go to math. Zeke is in the other fifth-grade class, and he had history.

"I'll bring it with me to lunch," I told him.

Lunchtime finally came and Zeke waved me over to a table in the corner where we could have some privacy. I pulled the cell phone out of my backpack and handed it to him.

"A *flip* phone?" he asked, chuckling. "Who gave this to you, Alexander Graham Bell?"

"Funny," I said. "I know. It's a relic."

"They probably had phones like this when Houdini was alive," Zeke cracked. "Who gave it to you?"

"I don't know," I told him. "I found it with all the flowers and candy and stuff in my room when I was in the hospital. There was no note or anything with it."

"Maybe your mom gave it to you," Zeke guessed. "After what happened to you, maybe she wants you to have a cell phone so you can reach her in an emergency."

"It wasn't my mom," I said. "She told me just last week that she didn't think I was ready for a cell phone. And if she *did* give me one, she would've said something."

"You didn't tell her about this, right?" Zeke asked.

"No way. Not yet."

"Well, that's good," Zeke said, handing the cell phone back to me. "Turn it on."

"I *can't* turn it on," I told him. "The battery's dead. It died last night while I was texting with the Houdini impersonator."

"Then we need to get a charger for it, or a new battery," Zeke said. "How much money do you have on you?"

After school, Zeke and I walked down Broadway until we found a little store with a sign in the window that said they fix new and used cell phones.

"May I help you?" a teenage girl with purple hair and a pierced nose asked when we walked in.

"I need to buy a cell phone charger," I told her, pulling the phone out of my backpack. She looked at it, turning it over in her hand.

"Wow, are you kiddin' me?" she asked. "My mother used to have one like this a *long* time ago. They haven't sold these in years. I don't think they *make* chargers or batteries for these anymore."

"I know," I replied. "I just thought I'd give it a shot."

"Why don't you just get a *new* cell phone?" she asked. "We have a bunch you can look at. You can't even get online with this one. Don't the kids at your school make fun of you for carrying this thing around?"

I didn't want to explain the whole story about Houdini. She would never believe it.

"It's complicated," I told her. "But I need a charger for *this* one. It's kind of important."

She looked at me like I was a little crazy.

"It's a retro thing," Zeke told her. "Like listening to vinyl records. All the cool kids are getting into flip phones now."

"Just ignore him," I told her. "I need to charge it up to see if it works."

"Have you tried eBay?" she asked. "You might find old phone chargers there. Sorry I can't help, you guys."

Bummer.

"Maybe we should try Craigslist first," Zeke

said as we were about to open the door to leave. But the girl with the purple hair was calling to us.

"Hey, wait a minute," she said. "I just remembered. We have this junk drawer. Follow me."

She led us to the back of the store, where she opened up a big drawer and said we could rummage around in there as long as we liked. It was a mess, like a graveyard of old cell phones and cell phone parts. There were a bunch of chargers in there. I tried a few with jacks that didn't fit into my phone. But the fourth or fifth one seemed to fit.

"That doesn't mean it's gonna charge the thing," Zeke told me. "But it might."

"I hope it does," I replied as I took out my wallet. "It's gonna cost a lot of money. I bet these things are hard to find."

All I had in my wallet was a ten-dollar bill and two fives.

"How much do I owe you?" I asked the girl with purple hair.

"Take it," she said, waving my money away. "I feel sorry for you, carrying that antique around in broad daylight. Nobody else is gonna want the charger."

"Hey, thanks!"

"No prob," she said. "Come back when you're ready to get a phone from *this* century."

We went back to Zeke's house so my mom wouldn't see what we were doing. He plugged the charger into the wall outlet in his room and plugged my phone into the charger.

"It may not work," Zeke said. "But at least it didn't cost you anything."

A little red light went on and the screen lit up, which I took to be a good sign. Zeke knows his way around cell phones. He said it might take hours for the phone to get a full charge, but in the meantime we should be able to use it. That is, if it worked.

"Let's check the texts," he said as he fumbled with the little rubber keypad. "Any old texts you sent or received should still be here."

But they weren't. He poked around, trying all kinds of stuff, but he couldn't retrieve the texts from the previous night. They were gone.

"Maybe we can trace the *source* of the

texts," Zeke said. "If we can find out the number where they came from, it might help us find out who was sending them to you."

He fiddled with the keypad, but again, nothing. The memory had been wiped clean. It was like the flip phone had never been used.

"It's scrubbed," Zeke said, "Nothin' there."

"Bummer."

"Are you *sure* you're not messed up in the head since the coma?" Zeke asked. "That stuff happens, y'know. You could be brain damaged, like all those football players who got multiple concussions. I'm *serious*."

I felt myself getting angry at Zeke.

"So you don't believe me," I said sadly.

"Sure I believe you, man!" Zeke replied. "I just think that maybe you should talk to a shrink or somebody."

"I'm *fine*," I insisted, my voice going up a little. "I didn't imagine it! I had a long text conversation on this phone with *somebody*. I'm not saying it was the real Houdini, but he knew everything about Houdini. That's a fact."

I caught Zeke smirking. He thought I was

crazy. And I couldn't blame him, really. The whole thing *was* crazy. You can't communicate with dead people through a cell phone! I wasn't even sure you could communicate with live people with *this* cell phone. Maybe Zeke was right. Maybe I *was* hallucinating.

Zeke wasn't ready to give up just yet. He tried calling his own cell phone from my flip phone, but the call wouldn't go through. He would have liked to try calling the flip phone from his cell phone, but neither of us knew the number.

"This thing is a piece of junk," Zeke said, tossing the phone to me. "You might as well throw it away. Or bring it back to the cell phone store. Maybe they can recycle it for parts. But I doubt it. Maybe you should take it to an antique store. It might be worth something as a collectible."

So that was that. That was the end of it. I went home.

"What did you do after school today?" my mom asked when I got home.

"I went over Zeke's," I told her.

"And what did you do there?"

"Nothin'," I said.

After dinner I went upstairs and stuck the cell phone and charger back in my night-table drawer. I did my homework and watched a few YouTube videos on my laptop. I was just about to drop off to sleep, when...

Bzzzzz...bzzzzz...bzzzzz...

I was alert immediately. I lunged for the drawer and took out the phone. The screen was lit up. There was one word on the screen....

"HARRY?"

I just stared at it for a long time. I didn't know what to do.

"ARE YOU THERE?" it said on the screen.

"Who is this?" I tapped.

"IT'S ME. HOUDINI."

LIFE IS SHORT.
DEATH IS FOREVER

I half believed it. Who knows? Maybe it really *was* Houdini. Maybe he *was* texting me from the afterlife.

Oh, that's just crazy. It couldn't be. I don't believe in that stuff.

I decided to humor him. That's how detectives work, right? Maybe I could trap him and find out who he—or she—really is. But before I could send him another message...

"WHERE WERE YOU?" appeared on my little screen. I noticed for the first time that the person who was texting me always wrote in capital letters.

"I had to charge up the cell phone," I tapped.

While I waited for a reply, I plugged the phone and charger into the wall outlet so the phone would get a full charge and not run out of juice in the middle of our text conversation, the way it did last time.

"WHAT IS A CELL PHONE?" came the reply.

"How are you communicating with me?" I tapped. "Are you using a computer?"

"A WHAT?"

"A computer," I tapped. "It's sort of like a smart calculator."

"WHAT IS A CALCULATOR?"

Oh yeah. There were no cell phones, computers, *or* calculators in 1926, the year Houdini died. Television didn't even exist yet back then. If he was pranking me, this guy was *good*.

"Never mind," I tapped. "How are you communicating with me?"

"I CANNOT EXPLAIN," was the reply. "I JUST AM."

Well, that wasn't very helpful.

"Let me ask you this question," I tapped. "WHY are you communicating with me?"

"I WANT TO KNOW HOW THE WORLD HAS CHANGED SINCE MY DEATH."

Hmmm. I wouldn't say that history is my best subject in school. But I know the basics, of course. I tried to think of the important events that had happened since 1926. I remembered learning that the big stock market crash was in 1929, just three years after Houdini died.

"There was the Great Depression," I tapped, "and after that was over we had a world war."

"WE ALREADY HAD A WORLD WAR," came the reply. "IN 1914. IT WAS THE WAR TO END ALL WARS."

"Well, we had another one," I tapped. "We've had a few more, actually—Korea, Vietnam, Iraq—but they weren't world wars. Let me see. They invented jet planes that could fly really fast, and atomic bombs that could wipe out entire cities. Oh, and we landed some guys on the moon."

"YOU ARE JOKING, RIGHT?"

"No, it happened for real," I tapped, "back in 1969. Then there was terrorism and lots of school shootings after the turn of the century. And the World Trade Center attack on 9/11."

"WHAT IS A WORLD TRADE CENTER?"

Of course. The World Trade Center hadn't been *built* when Houdini was alive. The Empire State Building didn't even exist yet. It must have been a completely different New York a hundred years ago.

"The World Trade Center was two really tall office buildings in New York City," I tapped, trying to make things as simple as possible. "Somebody flew planes into them and knocked them down."

"HOW IS MY HOUSE?" he replied, changing the subject. He remembered from our last conversation that I live in his house on 113th Street. At least I knew I was texting with the same person.

"Fine," I tapped. "My mother takes good care of it."

"NOT YOUR FATHER?"

"He died when I was a baby," I tapped.

"I AM SORRY. MY FATHER ALSO DIED WHEN I WAS YOUNG. TAKE GOOD CARE OF YOUR MOTHER. SHE IS ALL YOU HAVE."

I knew all about Houdini's mother. He worshipped her. After she died, he got interested in spiritualism. He desperately wanted to communicate with his mother. But when he held séances with people who claimed to be mediums, he realized they were all con artists. That's when he started denouncing spiritualism.

"Have you reached your mother?" I tapped. "I mean, since you're both dead and everything?"

"NO. BUT HERE I AM COMMUNICATING WITH YOU. LIFE IS FUNNY THAT WAY. SO IS DEATH."

"I'm sorry," I tapped, not knowing what else to say.

"I MISS MY HOUSE," he replied.

He went on to describe specific things he

missed about the house. Like the eight-foot mirror in the bathroom where he would rehearse his magic tricks, and the oversize sunken bathtub where he would practice holding his breath for long periods of time.

"I REMEMBER THE FLOORBOARD NEXT TO THE BED ON THE THIRD FLOOR," he texted. "EVERY TIME I PUT MY FOOT DOWN, IT MADE A CREAKY NOISE."

What?! That's *my* room! It finally dawned on me. For the first time, I believed that he was telling the truth. It was real. Harry Houdini was actually texting me from the afterlife.

"It's really you, isn't it?" I tapped.

"YES. I HAVE BEEN TRYING TO TELL YOU THAT."

I noticed that the hairs on my forearms were standing up. I was actually exchanging texts with a dead guy.

"What does it feel like...to be dead?" I tapped.

"IT IS HARD TO EXPLAIN," Houdini replied, "THERE ARE SOME GOOD THINGS."

Houdini went on to tell me a few of the

advantages of no longer being alive. Like, when you're dead, you don't get sick or hurt. You don't have to brush your teeth or wash your hands or think about your hair turning gray and falling out as you get older. You don't have to deal with the inconveniences of life. Paying bills. Shoveling snow. Deciding what to eat for dinner. You just exist.

"IT IS SOMEWHAT LIBERATING TO BE FREE OF THE HUMAN BODY," he explained.

"Do you feel cold?" I tapped. "I mean, with your body being underground and everything."

I knew that Houdini was buried in a cemetery in Queens, just a subway ride away. I had been meaning to go out there sometime to see his gravesite, but I never got around to it.

"ONLY MY PHYSICAL BODY IS BURIED," he replied. "IT IS JUST A BUNCH OF BONES. MY SPIRIT IS EVERYWHERE."

"If your spirit is everywhere, then it must be in my room," I tapped. "Are you watching me right now?"

There was a pause, as if he was thinking it over. And then...

"YES."

It was a little creepy, I must admit, knowing that Harry Houdini—and maybe other dead people—were able to see me when I couldn't see them. I looked around my room for something that nobody in the world would be able to see. I opened the junk drawer at my bedside and pulled out a ruler.

"What am I holding in my hand?" I tapped.

"A RULER."

That clinched it. It *was* Houdini. It *had* to be Houdini.

The hairs on my arm stood up again. It was thrilling to know that the spirit of the great Harry Houdini was right there with me in my room.

"Can I touch you?" I tapped, as I waved a hand in the air over my bed.

"NO," Houdini replied. "IT DOESN'T WORK THAT WAY."

I thought I heard my mom walking down the hall from her bedroom, but it was just some noise outside.

I was having fun swapping texts with

Houdini. I didn't want it to end. I sensed that Houdini was in no rush to leave either.

"Can you tell me more secrets of your magic?" I tapped.

"SURE. IT DOESN'T MATTER ANYMORE. DO YOU WANT TO BE A MAGICIAN WHEN YOU GROW UP?"

It had crossed my mind. I had also thought about becoming a scientist, or maybe a video-game designer. But being a magician could be pretty cool.

"Maybe," I tapped.

For the next fifteen minutes or so, Houdini gave me a text tutorial on what he called "escapology"—the science of escape. It was like he needed to get something off his chest. Maybe he was looking for somebody to follow in his footsteps.

He told me that when you have people tie you up, you should always use one long rope rather than a bunch of small ropes. Why? Because a long rope will have more slack to it, which you can use to escape. He also said to always spit on your wrists before you get tied up. It helps you slip off the ropes. Oh, and he said he could undo knots with his toes. He was able to use his toes the way regular people used their fingers.

He told me what to do when your hands are tied behind your back. You just bend forward and get your arms down over your hips until your hands are just behind your knees. Then sit on the floor with your legs crossed. Take each foot out through your looped arms, one at a time. That will bring your wrists in front of your body, where you can use your teeth to untie the knots. It's not easy, Houdini explained, but it works. He encouraged me to try it.

He told me the trick to getting out of six or seven handcuffs is to make sure the easier ones were put on near your wrists and the harder ones closer to your elbows, where your arms are thicker. That way, you can break out of the easy ones first, and then just slip your arms through the harder ones.

Oh, and he said that whenever he escaped from a pair of handcuffs, he would ask if he could keep them as a souvenir. He would take them apart and file the insides down to make them easier to open next time. Then he'd plant them with people in the audience at his next show. Most people didn't bring handcuffs to his shows, so he would just provide ones that were easy to escape from.

"Why would I need to know any of that?" I tapped.

"YOU NEVER KNOW WHEN IT MIGHT COME IN HANDY," he replied. "AND NEVER MAKE A TRICK LOOK EASY. IF IT LOOKS EASY, THE AUDIENCE WON'T BE IMPRESSED. LET THEM SEE YOU STRUGGLE. MAKE IT LOOK HARD. PEOPLE WON'T CARE IF IT LOOKS EASY."

There was more, but I think you get the idea.

"DO YOU WANT TO KNOW THE BIGGEST SECRET TO MY SUCCESS?" Houdini texted.

"Yes!" I tapped excitedly.

"WE ALL ARE AFRAID OF SOMETHING," he texted. "EVEN THE RICHEST, MOST

POWERFUL PERSON IN THE WORLD HAS FEAR. BUT IF I COULD BE TIED UP, SHACKLED, AND ESCAPE FROM A BOX THAT WAS THROWN INTO A RIVER, PEOPLE FEEL THEY CAN ESCAPE FROM THE THING THEY FEAR. I GAVE PEOPLE HOPE. THAT WAS MY POWER."

Wow. It took me a minute to process all that.

But Houdini wasn't finished texting. "WHAT DO YOU FEAR?" he asked.

I thought it over. The usual fears many people have—insects, blood, loud noises, scary monsters under the bed—never bothered me.

"Bullies," I finally tapped. There's this kid named Simon Foster at school who has been hassling me since second grade. "And heights. I don't like high places."

Ever since I was little, I got a weird feeling whenever I was in a tall building, or walking over a bridge. And I don't like being in elevators.

"YOU CANNOT GET PAST FEAR UNLESS YOU CONFRONT IT," Houdini replied. "THEN

YOU REJECT FEAR. IF YOU CAN DO THAT, YOU CAN ACCOMPLISH WHAT APPEARS TO BE IMPOSSIBLE."

Houdini had given me a lot of stuff to think about.

"Thank you," I tapped. "It is nice of you to give me so much of your time."

"I HAVE NOTHING BUT TIME," he replied. "LIFE IS SHORT, BUT DEATH IS FOREVER."

I was beginning to sense a certain sadness in Houdini's texts. Maybe he was spending so much time texting with me because he was lonely. And I suppose eternity can be boring.

It was getting late. I had to get up for school in the morning.

"I have to go," I tapped. "Can I text you again sometime?"

"I'M SORRY, NO. THE LIVING CANNOT CONTACT THE DEAD. IT IS A ONE-WAY STREET. ONLY THE DEAD CAN CONTACT THE LIVING. THAT IS ANOTHER ONE OF THE ADVANTAGES OF BEING DEAD."

"Okay," I tapped. "But I really want to do this again. There's so much more I want to ask you. Like, how did you escape from a straitjacket? Stuff like that."

"TOMORROW NIGHT," was the reply.

FRIENDS AND ENEMIES

The largest church in the country is three blocks from my house. It's the Cathedral Church of St. John the Divine. The thing is huge, and one of the windows is made out of ten thousand pieces of stained glass. But here's the most amazing thing about the church—there are peacocks living in the parking lot.

I kid you not. The peacocks' names are Phil, Jim, and yes...Harry. No, Harry wasn't named after me *or* Harry Houdini. He was named after a priest. Peacocks have been living at the church since the 1980s, when they were donated by the Bronx Zoo. Here's the church…

And here's Phil...

Anyway, Zeke and I sometimes stop by to
visit Phil, Jim, and Harry on our way home

from school. They're not all that friendly. You're not supposed to feed them or touch them, but it's kind of cool to see peacocks running around in the middle of New York City.

"You want to come over tonight and hang out?" Zeke asked as we watched Phil and Jim trudge around the driveway.

"I can't," I told him. "I gotta do something."

It wasn't like me to be secretive around Zeke. But he had already told me he thought I was crazy to think that dead people can communicate with the living. I didn't want to tell him I couldn't go over his house because I had an appointment to text with Harry Houdini again.

I couldn't stop thinking about my text session the night before. Houdini had chosen *me*, of all the living people in the world, to communicate with. I had a delicious secret. I felt special. I wanted to share it with Zeke, but I was a little embarrassed.

"Don't tell me," Zeke said. "You heard from your new BFF again, didn't you?"

"Yeah," I admitted.

I finally told Zeke about my chat with Houdini, and how I became convinced that he was for real when he mentioned the creaky floorboard in my bedroom. I made Zeke promise not to blab it all over school. The last thing I needed was for the kids to find out and start making fun of me. I told Zeke not to tell his parents. I probably shouldn't even have told *him*.

"Do you have the flip phone with you?" Zeke asked me.

"Yup."

I sure did. After my last session with Houdini, I had decided to carry the flip phone with me at all times. Who knew when Houdini might decide to get in touch with me? He said he was going to text that night. But what time zone was Houdini in? Do the spirits of the dead even *have* time zones? They're everywhere. They might not even know what day or night means.

I patted my right back pocket, where I had carefully stashed the phone. If I lost it or if anything happened to it, that would be a disaster. No more conversations with Houdini. My phone was his link to our time.

"Are you gonna let *me* meet Houdini?" Zeke asked. I looked at him to see if he was putting me on.

"Maybe," I replied. "After he and I get to know each other a little better maybe."

"Did he say he is in heaven?" Zeke asked. "Is he in hell? Where do you think he is?"

"I don't know," I told him. "He told me he's everywhere. But we didn't get into much of that stuff. Maybe the next time I text with him."

"When will that be?"

"Tonight," I told Zeke. "That's why I can't hang out with you."

"It's okay."

It didn't look like Zeke was okay. He looked a little hurt.

"Do you believe me?" I asked him. "You believe me, don't you?"

Zeke wouldn't give me a yes or a no. He just shook his head sadly from side to side. I took that to mean no.

"I'm really not sure, dude," Zeke said. "It's

hard for me to believe in stuff I can't see with my own eyes. But let's say it really *is* Houdini. Why do you think he's communicating with *you*?"

"He told me he wanted to know what happened in the world after he died," I told Zeke. "But I think it's more than that. He must have a pretty important message he wants me to deliver. Either that, or he's just lonely. What do *you* think?"

"You really want to know?" Zeke asked.

"Yeah."

"I think you both have daddy issues," he told me.

Oh, here we go. Zeke's mom is a psychologist, so naturally he thinks he knows what makes everybody tick.

"Let's hear it," I said.

"You don't have a dad," Zeke explained. "You never knew your dad because he died when you were so young. So Houdini is a father figure to you."

I snorted.

"And you think *I'm* crazy?" I said.

"Hear me out," Zeke told me. "Houdini and his wife never had children, right? So maybe he has baby issues. You're a child. So it's like you're his new child and he's your new dad. It fits. That's my theory."

"That's ridiculous," I replied.

Zeke has been my best friend for a long time. We like the same teams, the same bands. He and I were always in synch on most stuff. Until now. I didn't want to lose his friendship. But I was feeling some anger bubbling up inside on both sides.

"You're just jealous," I told him. "That's what I think."

"Jealous of what?" Zeke asked.

"You're jealous of Houdini," I said. "It bothers you that I'm spending time with him instead of with you. You're afraid that he's my new best friend."

"Maybe he's your *imaginary* friend," Zeke replied.

I wished Houdini would have texted me at that moment. Then Zeke would know I wasn't crazy.

I'll tell you what else I think. I didn't tell Zeke this, but I think he feels guilty over what happened at the Freedom Tunnel. It was *his* idea to put the coins on the track. He feels he's responsible for me getting hurt that day and nearly dying. So if I suffered brain damage or went crazy after hitting my head at the railroad tracks, Zeke thinks it's his fault. But I'm not crazy. I'm not brain damaged. Houdini really *did* communicate with me. I'm not hallucinating. It really happened.

"I gotta go home," Zeke said abruptly.

We didn't say goodbye. I watched him walk away without turning around.

I spent a few minutes watching the peacocks, but it wasn't that much fun without Zeke so I decided to leave too. To get home from St. John the Divine, I either walk to the front and go down 110th Street, or walk out the back and go through Morningside Park, which is faster, and prettier.

I decided to go through the park.

It was a mistake.

There's this really long staircase that goes down into Morningside Park. This is what it looks like.

It's 155 steps. Yeah, I counted them. I was somewhere in the middle when I heard my name.

"Hey, Mancini!"

I knew who it was. Simon Foster, that jerk in my school who has been picking on me ever since we were in second grade. I don't know what Simon's problem is. He probably has a bad home situation or something. But hey, my dad died when I was two. I had a bad home situation, and I didn't become a jerk like Simon.

He came out of the bushes at the side of the stairs, as if he had been hiding there waiting for me. He blocked my way. I couldn't go past him. If I tried to run back up the steps, he would tackle me from behind.

I glanced left and right quickly. There had to be somebody else around who would see this. It's a busy park. But no. Simon always made sure of that. Bullies always manage to get you when you're alone.

Why couldn't this have happened five

minutes before? Simon never would have messed with me if Zeke had been around. It would have been two against one. Simon probably saw Zeke come down the steps and figured I'd be heading home the same way.

I thought that maybe if I didn't make eye contact with Simon, he'd leave me alone. Wishful thinking.

"Well, well, well," he said, a stupid smirk on his face.

Simon is bigger than me. Not much bigger, but big enough to win a fight with me. Not that I know how to fight. When I was little, my mother suggested I take karate lessons. I talked her into letting me take a magic class instead.

"What do you want, Simon?" I asked, knowing full well what he wanted.

"For starters, you could loan me five bucks," Simon replied.

Loan him. Ha! As if I would ever see that money again.

"I don't have five bucks," I lied.

I knew I had twenty dollars in my pocket, because that's what I was prepared to pay for my cell phone charger before the lady in the store gave it to me for free. But why should I give my money to Simon? Grown-ups are always telling us that we should stand up for ourselves. Simon had no right to take my money.

"All I find I keep?" Simon asked.

Oh, the classic "all I find I keep" line. Bullies have been using that one for centuries, I bet. They make it seem like it's *your* fault that they're robbing you.

Simon reached for my pants pockets, and I slapped his hand away. That got him mad, and he grabbed my hand.

If I was really cool, I would have kneed him in the face when he leaned over to reach for my pocket. Then I would have jammed my elbow into the back of his head to make him fall forward, tumble back down the steps, and beg for mercy when I'd come after him for more.

But I'm not really cool.

"Get your hands off me!" I shouted as

he tried to get at my pockets with his other hand.

"So you *do* have five bucks," Simon said. "I knew you were a liar, Mancini."

Yeah, I'm a liar. So I guess he's entitled to take my money.

I didn't care about the money. He could take my money. But I didn't want him to find my flip phone. What a dope I was to carry it around with me all day. I protected my right back pocket.

Simon grabbed my arm and twisted it. He put his other hand over my mouth so I couldn't call out for help. I struggled to get free, but he was too strong for me.

"Don't make this hard on yourself, Mancini," he said. "It's just five bucks."

"Let go!" I tried to shout.

I stomped on his foot hard, and I guess that took him by surprise because he released his grip on my arm. He wasn't used to me fighting back. I usually just give him the money.

He was really mad now. He wrapped his

right arm tightly around my chest and was grabbing at my back pockets.

"There must be something pretty valuable in here or you wouldn't be fighting so hard," he mumbled into my ear.

I tried to cover my right pocket with my hand, but he got to it first. He reached in and pulled out my flip phone. As soon as he got a look at it, he let go of me and doubled over laughing.

"Are you kidding me?" he said, barely able to control himself. "*This* is what you were fighting for?"

"Give it back, Simon!" I shouted, pretending to be assertive.

"What are you gonna do with this," he asked. "Call the 1990s?"

Then he opened the phone and pretended to talk into it.

"Hello 1990s?" he asked. "I have one of your cell phones. Do you need it?"

"Give it *back*, Simon!" I shouted.

"Maybe I will and maybe I won't," he said. "Maybe if you give me the five bucks I politely asked for, I'll give back your antique phone."

I thought about giving him the five bucks. I could just give him the money and he'd give me my phone back. What's the big deal? I was going to pay more than five bucks for the phone charger anyway. But I just couldn't do it this time. It was the principle of the thing.

"No," I said firmly, trying to snatch the phone out of his hand. He yanked it away.

"Okay, then *nobody* gets it," Simon said. He reared back and heaved the phone into the woods.

"Noooooo!" I shouted.

I desperately tried to follow the trajectory of the phone until it landed in some bushes. Then I ran off in that direction.

"Ha!" Simon said. "Play fetch, Mancini."

Simon walked away, cackling the whole time like the jerk he is.

I spent about a half an hour searching through the bushes. It wasn't easy, because the ground is really steep. Also, the sun was getting lower in the sky and it was starting to get dark out. I didn't think I would ever find my phone. But finally, miraculously, I kicked a clump of leaves and there it was. I grabbed it and tapped the power button.

Thankfully, it turned on.

METAMORPHOSIS

I spent a lot of time working on my math homework when I got home, but I just couldn't focus on it. I was thinking about Houdini the whole time. He told me he was going to contact me that night, but I didn't know when.

The more I thought about texting with Houdini, the more I thought how crazy it all was. Maybe Zeke was right. Maybe Houdini was some kind of imaginary father figure to me. Maybe I was the son he never had. Maybe I was crazy.

And then, just before ten o'clock...

Bzzzzz...bzzzzz...bzzzzz...

Yes!

I yanked open the drawer of my night table and grabbed the flip phone.

"HARRY?" it said on the screen.

It still freaked me out that he just called me "Harry." I thought about calling Zeke and telling him to come over to my house right away. It would be great if he could witness one of my text sessions with Houdini. *Then* he would know I'm not making it all up. But it would be too risky to call Zeke. I'd have to go downstairs, make the call on our landline, and explain to my mother why I needed to have Zeke come over so late at night. I decided against it.

"I'm here," I tapped on the keypad.

"REMEMBER ME?" Houdini texted.

"Of course," I tapped. I thought of adding an exclamation mark at the end, but I didn't want to let him know how excited I was.

"DO PEOPLE REMEMBER ME?"

That threw me. He *really* wanted to be remembered. It seemed important to him. And Houdini *was* remembered. He's been dead for close to a hundred years, but whenever somebody walks by my house and sees the plaque by the front door, they tell me they know who he was. Even little kids know about the great Harry Houdini. He was sort of like Elvis, JFK, and Marilyn Monroe. Everybody knows who they were even though they've been gone for a long time.

Houdini's name had even entered the language. When you say that somebody "pulled a Houdini," everybody knows it means he or she escaped from a seemingly inescapable situation.

"Everybody remembers you," I tapped.

A pause. And then . . .

"HOW IS LIFE?"

"Okay," I tapped.

I thought about asking him "How is death?" But that would have been obnoxious.

Little by little, we were getting to know each other. It wasn't like Houdini to make small talk. I had the sense that he had a message to deliver, or there was something he wanted me to do for him.

"BUT LIFE COULD BE BETTER, RIGHT?" he texted.

"I guess," I tapped.

Sure. Life can *always* be better. My mom could win the lottery. That would make life better. I could become the centerfielder for the Mets. That would make life better. What was he driving at? My screen was blank for a while, and then...

"WHAT DO YOU WANT TO ESCAPE FROM?"

Weird question. What was he talking about? Handcuffs? Jail cells? I didn't want to escape from anything.

"Huh?" I tapped.

"EVERYBODY WANTS TO ESCAPE FROM SOMETHING," he texted. "IT'S HUMAN NATURE. WE ARE NEVER SATISFIED WITH WHAT WE HAVE IN THE PRESENT. MAN HAS ALWAYS DREAMED OF ESCAPING FROM WHERE HE IS PRESENTLY."

Houdini's words kept scrolling up my screen....

"FREEDOM AND LIBERTY ARE WHAT AMERICA IS ALL ABOUT," he said. "WHEN I DID AN ESCAPE, IT GAVE PEOPLE HOPE. IT MADE THEM BELIEVE THEY COULD ESCAPE FROM THEIR DISMAL LIVES."

I didn't know how to respond. My life wasn't dismal. I was pretty happy, actually. I felt like tapping out "What's your point?" But again, that would seem obnoxious.

"THERE IS ONLY ONE THING I COULD NOT ESCAPE FROM," he texted.

"What was that?" I tapped.

"DEATH," he texted. "I SPENT MY LIFE ESCAPING FROM DEATH. BUT WHEN IT CAME FOR ME, THERE WAS NO WAY TO ESCAPE."

Now he was creeping me out. I decided not to reply. I'd wait and see what else he had to say. But he didn't text anything more. I stared at the blank screen on my phone. Finally, I couldn't resist responding.

"Why did you contact me?" I finally tapped.

"THERE IS SOMETHING THAT I WANT TO DISCUSS WITH YOU," he texted.

Aha. It was about time he got to the point.

"What?" I tapped.

"METAMORPHOSIS."

I knew that word. It's a fancy way to say "change." I had learned in science class that many animal species in the world go through some kind of metamorphosis during their lifetime. Caterpillars change into butterflies. Tadpoles change into frogs. But I also knew that Houdini wasn't talking about the metamorphosis of an animal species.

Metamorphosis was one of Houdini's earliest and most famous tricks. He began performing it with his wife Bess back in 1895. It was a big part of his act for the next thirty years.

Here's how it worked:

A trunk was hauled out onto the stage. You know what I mean by a trunk, right? It's not a suitcase. It's bigger. The trunk was more than big enough to hold a man. Houdini would open the trunk and climb into a large black flannel

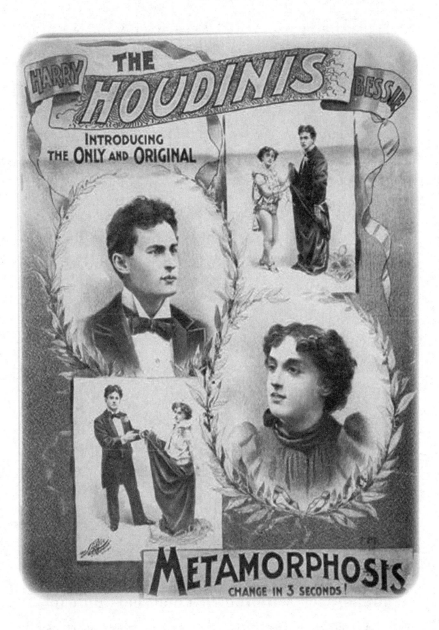

sack that was inside. Bess would put heavy tape over Houdini's mouth. Then she would tie Houdini's hands behind his back with rope. Bess would make a knot in the top of the sack and seal it with wax. Then she would close the trunk's lid. Then she would lock the trunk with six padlocks. Finally, she would wrap a rope around it and knot it tightly.

Simply escaping from the trunk would have been pretty remarkable, but what Houdini did was even *more* amazing.

Bess would wheel out a large curtain and place it in front of the trunk so the audience couldn't see it anymore. Then she would climb up on top of the trunk and clap her hands three times. On the third clap, the curtain would open, and instead of Bess standing on top of the trunk, it was Houdini!

To completely blow the audience's mind, Houdini would then jump down off the trunk and remove the rope, unlock the padlocks, and open the lid. Out popped Bess from inside the flannel sack, with the knot and seal unbroken.

How did they do it? Audiences were so

stunned by Metamorphosis that many times they didn't even applaud. It was sort of like when Houdini was locked in a trunk and thrown into the river. Nobody could explain how he escaped. The only logical explanation—and some people believed this—was that Harry and Bess had found a way to deconstruct the atoms of their bodies so they could switch places.

The most amazing thing about Metamorphosis is not that the Houdinis did it, but how *fast* they did it. The whole trick seemed to take just three seconds. One moment Bess was standing on top of the trunk with Houdini locked inside it, and a few seconds later Houdini was standing on top of the trunk with Bess inside the sack.

I had watched a bunch of magicians duplicate Metamorphosis on YouTube. You can watch them yourself. But I could never figure out how they pulled it off. Obviously it was a trick, but how was it done? How did they make the switch at all? How did they do it so fast? The trunk was padlocked and bound with ropes.

"What was the secret to Metamorphosis?" I tapped.

"SIMPLE," Houdini replied. "THE BOX HAD A REAR PANEL THAT OPENED INWARD. I'D CLIMB OUT OF THE BOX WHILE BESS WAS TALKING AND THEN BESS WOULD CLIMB IN."

Smart! If the panel opened *in*, it wouldn't affect the ropes that were wrapped around the trunk.

"But how did you get out of the sack and get Bess into it so fast?" I tapped.

"THERE WAS A SLIT IN THE BOTTOM OF THE SACK," he replied. "I WOULD CLIMB OUT WHILE BESS WAS LOCKING THE TRUNK AND SHE WOULD CLIMB IN WHILE I WAS UNLOCKING IT. THE TIMING HAD TO BE PERFECT."

"But what about the clapping?" I asked. "Bess clapped her hands three times, and then instantly she was in the box."

"THAT WASN'T BESS CLAPPING," Houdini texted. "IT WAS ME. BESS WAS ALREADY IN THE TRUNK BY THEN."

Of *course!*

Once you knew how a trick worked, it seemed so obvious. I slapped my forehead.

But what did Metamorphosis have to do with *me?* I wasn't going to go on a stage and get locked inside a trunk. I was about to tap in words to that effect when Houdini sent me another text....

"HOW WOULD YOU LIKE TO DO A METAMORPHOSIS?"

What? I couldn't imagine what he had in mind.

"That's impossible," I tapped. "We exist in different centuries."

"NOTHING IS IMPOSSIBLE," Houdini tapped right back. "YOU SHOULD KNOW THAT BY NOW."

Yeah, nothing is impossible...for *him.* For an average person, it sometimes seemed impossible to escape from the problems in his or her life. But Houdini could escape from *anything.* If he could escape from handcuffs and jail cells and padlocked trunks, maybe it made people believe they could escape from whatever was confining them. Poverty. Depression. Disease. Nothing was impossible.

I was finally beginning to put two and two together.

"Are you saying you want to switch places with me?" I tapped.

"YES."

Aha. At last I understood the real reason why Houdini had contacted me. It seemed crazy, but he wanted me to help him get out of the only thing he could never escape from.

He wanted to escape his own death.

"I...don't think that's such a good idea," I tapped.

"WHY NOT?" he texted. "YOU CAN BRING ME BACK. I DIED YOUNG. I WANT TO BE ALIVE AGAIN."

This was getting scary. I wanted to help the guy, but what if I did and Houdini was alive again? Would that be legal? What if I changed history for the worse? I was beginning to regret that I had ever communicated with Houdini in the first place. I didn't know what to do.

"I AM DESPERATE," he texted.

"I have to go," I tapped.

"DON'T!" he texted. "STOP! DON'T LEAVE ME HERE!"

He was freaking me out. Instinctively, I snapped the flip phone shut and hung up on him. I didn't want to deal with this right now. But a few seconds later...

Bzzzzz...bzzzzz...bzzzzz...

He wasn't going to give up. I thought about ignoring the text. What could he do? Come and get me? Make me disappear, like he famously did with an elephant in 1918?

Bzzzzz...bzzzzz...bzzzzz...

Against my better judgment, I opened the phone again.

"WE MUST HAVE HAD A BAD CONNECTION," he texted.

"So let me get this straight," I tapped. "You get to come to the 21st century. And what? I get to be dead? That doesn't sound like much fun to me."

"NO," he replied. "YOU DON'T GET TO BE DEAD. YOU GET TO BE ME!"

"Huh?" I finally tapped, after looking at the phone for a long time.

"DON'T YOU WANT TO BE THE MOST FAMOUS MAN IN THE WORLD?"

"I'm not sure."

That was the truth. I've often thought it would be cool to be a famous celebrity. But then, it would be a drag to have people following me around and asking me to sign autographs and stuff all the time. Who needs that aggravation?

"IT WOULD JUST BE TEMPORARY," Houdini texted.

"How long?" I tapped.

"ONE HOUR."

"So you would be in my century for one hour and I would be in your century for one hour?"

"EXACTLY," he texted. "I CAN MAKE THAT HAPPEN."

One hour. That didn't seem very long. It could be fun. That is, if he could pull it off.

"How do you do that?" I tapped.

"THROUGH METAMORPHOSIS. I AM HOUDINI, REMEMBER?"

It sounded like a lot of crap to me. How could he *possibly* send himself to my time and send me to his? But then, how was he texting me in the first place? It was like magic. He was a magician, after all. Nothing was impossible.

"When?" I tapped.

"THERE IS NO TIME LIKE THE PRESENT," he texted.

"Give me a minute," I tapped.

I needed to think things over. If we did a Metamorphosis right now, I would just be gone for an hour. Then I'd be back. My mother would never know I was gone. Nobody would know. I could just get up in the morning and go to school like nothing had happened. It could be cool. I'd have a memory to last a lifetime.

"What do I have to do?" I tapped.

"NOTHING," he texted. "HANG UP. LIE DOWN. LEAVE THE REST TO ME."

"Okay," I tapped. "I trust you. Goodbye."

"THANK YOU," he texted.

Why was I trusting him? I asked myself. *I didn't know this guy. Oh, what difference did it make? He probably can't do it anyway. What did I have to lose?*

I closed the phone and put it back in the drawer. This was it. I couldn't believe I was actually going to do it. It was risky, I knew. Maybe I would regret it. But my mom always told me you've got to take some risks in life if you want to get anywhere. You'll never remember all the times you played it safe and everything worked out fine. What you'll remember will be the times you took a risk and something good happened.

I lay down on my back and closed my eyes. I took a deep breath.

Nothing happened. Not at first. Maybe nothing was going to happen. Maybe Houdini didn't know how to do Metamorphosis after all.

And then I noticed a rumbling. An earthquake? My bed wasn't shaking. *I* was. It was very gentle at first, and gradually it became more powerful. It didn't hurt. It was sort of like one of those coin-operated vibrating chairs they have in airports and furniture stores.

I wanted to open my eyes to see what was happening to me, but I didn't dare. I didn't want to mess things up.

It felt like the room was spinning.

And then I was gone.

MISDIRECTION

When I opened my eyes, I was outdoors. It was daytime, and bright. I had to shield my eyes from the sun. I didn't know where I was. It didn't look like New York City.

There were people all around me. There must have been hundreds of them. And they were all staring at me, buzzing with conversation and excitement. I looked around quickly for clues. There were lots of tall buildings.

I was downtown in a big city somewhere, but I didn't know where. It sure didn't seem like the 21st century. All the men were wearing those old-time hats I'd seen in movies. Nobody wears those hats anymore.

I scanned the advertising signs: COFFEE 5 CENTS. CHEVROLET. BROMO-SELTZER. GAYETY THE-ATER. LOEW'S STATE. A movie theater was playing something called *The Cabinet of Dr. Caligari*. A street sign read MCGEE. I didn't remember any McGee Street in New York.

Three tall guys walked over to me. One wore glasses, and one had on some sort of military uniform. He had a pleasant smile on his face.

"Where am I?" I asked.

"Hahaha!" laughed the guy in the uniform. "Very funny."

He said it as if it was totally obvious where I was.

"Kansas City, of course," said the guy with glasses.

I noticed the big sign overhead—KANSAS CITY STAR. That must be the name of the local newspaper.

I looked down to see that I didn't have on my regular clothes. I was wearing a pair of striped pants, black shoes, a white shirt, and a jacket and tie. I would *never* have picked out these clothes. And I hate wearing a tie.

"Are you ready?" asked the guy in the uniform.

"Ready for *what*?" I asked.

He laughed again.

"What's happening?" I demanded. "What am I doing here? What year is it?"

"It's 1921, of course," said the guy with glasses.

So Houdini had *done* it. He had somehow pulled off Metamorphosis, just like he said he would, and sent me to Kansas City a hundred years in the past. I wondered where *he* was. Maybe he was sitting in my house at the same instant, watching my TV or playing with my computer.

I took a deep breath. I had known that Metamorphosis was going to happen, but it was still a shock to my system.

"Can I have a mirror?" I asked the guys.

"Get the man a mirror!" barked the guy in the military uniform. In seconds somebody hustled over with one of those little circular mirrors that ladies use to put on their makeup. He handed it to me and I looked at myself.

Oh no. I was Houdini.

My head was big, with piercing, penetrating blue-gray eyes that looked almost frightening. My hair was thick, bushy, and curly, and parted in the middle. My forehead was big, my eyebrows were wide, and my chin and cheekbones were sharp. I didn't look *anything* like the real me. And I was a grown man.

Not *that* grown. The three guys around me were all much bigger. I couldn't have been taller than five foot six. My legs seemed a little bowlegged. I knew Houdini was a short man. That was one of the advantages he had when it came to escaping from enclosed spaces.

"Are you okay, Mr. Houdini?" asked the guy in the uniform. "You look a little...under the weather."

"I need to sit down for just a moment," I said. "To catch my breath."

"Get Houdini a chair!" barked the guy in the uniform.

Somebody rushed over with a wooden folding chair.

I sat down heavily and put my head in my

hands, trying to clear it. How did I get into this? And how was I going to get back home?

As I was looking at the ground, I noticed a sheet of paper beneath my feet. I picked it up and flipped it over....

Oh no.

This was bad. This was *real* bad.

You may not even know what a straitjacket is. Houdini got his start by escaping from handcuffs and manacles. But after a few years people got bored watching that. They wanted something more exciting, and they didn't want to sit around for an hour waiting for him to open the handcuffs. So he started dreaming up other escapes. He was constantly trying to top himself to keep the public interested.

At some point, Houdini visited an insane asylum and saw inmates constrained in these heavy canvas "jackets." He knew immediately that could be his next escape.

A guy holding a big white megaphone addressed the crowd.

"Good afternoon, ladies and gentlemen," he announced. "Thanks to the good folks at the

Kansas City Star, I would like to welcome to our fair city the king of handcuffs, the master of manacles, the amazing Harry Houdini!"

The crowd erupted in applause and hat waving.

"For your entertainment and amazement," the megaphone man continued, "the great Houdini—who will be appearing at the Orpheum Theater tonight and tomorrow night—will perform—for free—for you—a feat which at one time was thought to be utterly impossible—that of escaping from a regulation straitjacket. Do you think he can do it?"

The crowd hollered back a chorus or yeses and nos.

"Well, there's only one way to find out," the megaphone man continued. "Stay right where you are. You will not want to miss this. Here is the greatest escapologist in the world, the man who makes the impossible possible. The one, the only, Harry…Houdini!"

More applause and hat waving.

I have to admit, it was kind of cool hearing

all those people cheering for me. I had never experienced anything like it. I felt very alive.

"Take a bow, Mr. Houdini," the guy in the military uniform whispered in my ear.

I stood up, bowed, and waved to the crowd. That made them cheer even louder.

But I was scared. I was also mad. Houdini never told me I'd have to do an escape as my part of Metamorphosis. He just said I would be the most famous man in the world. And now there was nothing I could do about it. It was a classic magician's misdirection.

The three guys helped me take off my jacket and tie. Then they picked up a strait-jacket and draped it over my shoulders back-ward, with the opening behind me.

"This is all a big mistake," I protested. "I'm not really Houdini. I'm just a kid."

"Hahaha," laughed the guy in the uniform. "You are a funny man, Mr. Houdini."

The straitjacket was made of very heavy brown canvas, with a leather collar and leather cuffs. The sleeves were about twice as long as regular sleeves, and sewn up to close off the

ends. It was like putting your arms into two cloth sacks.

The sleeves were overlapped so that my arms were crossed in front of me. At the end of each sleeve was a leather strap that wrapped around my body so the two sleeves met behind me and buckled in the back. Another strap was passed underneath, between my legs, and also buckled in the back. There were rivets at various points to prevent the fabric from being torn.

I was in big trouble. The only good thing about this escape, I suppose, was that I wouldn't have to pick a lock or hide a key inside any part of my body.

"This is all a mistake!" I said as two of the guys grabbed me in a bear hug while the other guy stuck his knee against my back so he could pull the straps as tight as possible. "Let me explain!"

The three of them laughed.

"Come on, Mr. Houdini," said the guy with glasses. "I know you've done this a hundred times before."

"But...but..."

I was wrapped up tight. This couldn't be happening! I had read a little bit about how Houdini escaped from straitjackets, but I never thought I would have to do it *myself*. How could I possibly get out of this situation?

While they were buckling me up, another guy came over lugging a long cable with a thick padded length of cloth at the end of it. He wrapped the cloth around my ankles and tied my legs together with it.

"What are you doing *that* for?" I asked.

"So we can hoist you up in the air, of course!" he replied.

"Wait. What?" I said, my voice rising. "You mean I've got to get out of this thing upside *down*?"

"Of course!" the guy said. "How else could all these people see you?"

"But…I'm afraid of heights," I said.

"Hahaha, very funny," said the guy in the military uniform.

"You know the drill, Houdini," said the guy with glasses.

I actually *did* know the drill. I had seen videos of Houdini doing this stunt on You-Tube. Usually, he performed his escapes behind a curtain so the audience couldn't see how he did it. The straitjacket escape was the only outdoor stunt he did in full view of an audience. It was his brother Hardeen, who was also a magician, who suggested it would be more dramatic if the audience could watch him struggle.

Oh, they were going to see a struggle all right.

"Maestro," shouted the guy with the big megaphone. "A little music, please!"

Somewhere, a band started playing. The guys lowered the upper part of my body down so I was lying on the ground. Somebody gave a signal, and the cable started slowly pulling my legs up.

The cable must have been attached to a pulley on the roof of the building. A guy down on the street was pulling me up. As my legs lifted off the ground, the guys held my upper body so that all my weight would not be on my head.

I closed my eyes. I was upside down now, being pulled up in the air. As more and more people could see me rising up, the crowd roared its approval.

"Help!" I shouted. "*Help!*"

People were laughing.

"I'm not joking!" I shouted. "Get me *out* of here!"

I could feel myself rising higher and higher. I could already feel the blood rushing to my head. When I opened my eyes, I could see windows of the office building filled with people.

I was about the same level as the Kansas City Star sign, nine stories up. That was on purpose, I'm sure. Photographers were leaning out of the windows, trying to get a shot of me with the sign in the background. I was just hanging there.

That's when I started to cry. I couldn't help it. It just came over me. I don't think the people below could see it. But I was helpless. Useless. And scared. I couldn't even move my arms to wipe the tears away. They collected in my eyebrows.

I tried to remember some of the things Houdini had texted me: "We are all afraid of something. You cannot get past fear unless you confront it. If you can do that, you can accomplish what appears to be impossible."

I looked down. There must have been *thousands* of people below, craning their necks to look up at me. They were standing so tightly together that none of them would have been able to sit down if they wanted to. I could also see lots of old old-time cars and trolleys, plus a few horse and buggies scattered around the blocks surrounding the Kansas City Star building. People were leaning out of windows waving, perched precariously on ledges, and wrapped around telephone poles.

I remembered something else Houdini had texted me.

"If I can escape," he said, "people feel they can escape from the thing they fear. I gave people hope."

Snap out of it, I told myself. I had to get past my fear of heights and face it.

It was time to get to work. I knew from reading books that one of the ways Houdini got out of a straitjacket was to intentionally dislocate his shoulder. Well, I wasn't about to do *that*. I was going to have to get out of the thing on my own.

I pushed my arms out against the strait-jacket as hard as I could, grunting from the effort.

Nothing. That got me nowhere, as expected. The straitjacket was wrapped pretty tightly. But even so, there was just a *little* slack in the cloth. That, I knew, was another one of Houdini's secrets. As they were putting a strait-jacket on him, he would take a deep breath to expand his chest as much as he could. At the same time, he would hunch his shoulders and hold his arms just a *little* bit away from his sides. That gave him a tiny bit of slack to work with, and that was all he needed.

Instinctively, I had done the same thing when they put the straitjacket on me. So when I expelled all the air in my lungs, there was some slack in the cloth. Using as much power as I could muster, I pushed my elbows down against my knees to get a little more room to allow me to lift my arms up.

I jammed my right elbow upward until it was closer to my face. I figured that if I could get one arm near my head, I might be able to unbuckle a strap with my teeth. I was already sweating and exhausted from struggling.

"You can do it, Houdini!" somebody shouted from below. "You can do *anything*!"

It occurred to me that being upside down may have actually been an advantage. Gravity made it easier for me to push my arm above my head. I somehow managed to force one elbow to the top of the straitjacket. Once my wrist was close enough to my face, I got to work loosening the buckle with my teeth.

It wasn't easy. The rope was twisting while I was thrashing and bending from the waist. I knew I was running out of time. I could feel the blood rushing to my head. Soon, I knew, I would become unconscious.

I was grunting, sweating, and flailing as I worked on the buckle with my mouth. The crowd below was loving it, yelling and screaming and urging me on. They seemed to enjoy watching me struggle.

I remembered what Houdini had texted me about escape. Everybody wants to escape from something. Human beings all want something different than what we have, something *better*. I guess that's what motivated us to send a man to the moon, to cure diseases, to invent new machines, or simply to get a better job and earn more money to make our lives easier. We all want to escape from who we are. Then we get to a new place and want to escape from *there*.

I managed to get the first buckle open with my teeth. But the wind was picking up, which caused the cable to sway back and forth like a pendulum. On each swing, I was getting dangerously close to a concrete window ledge. My head almost banged against it. The crowd gasped every time I swung close to the edge.

Houdini probably *loved* when this happened, I figured. Me, I hated every second of it.

I kept on grunting, sweating, and flailing around wildly as I worked to free my arms. Finally, after what felt like twenty minutes but was probably closer to ten, I was able to jerk my head and neck to get my arms out of the jacket. At that point, I could reach my back. Even though my hands were still trapped

in the sleeves, I was able to feel through the sleeves to work on the other buckles. One by one, I got them loose.

That was it! I ripped the jacket off my body and held my arms out on both sides like a cross. The crowd went nuts.

Finally, with a flourish, I dropped the straitjacket into the crowd below. There was cheering like I had never heard in my life.

I don't remember what happened after that. I must have passed out.

METAMORPHOSIS, PART II

Then I had a dream. I *think* it was a dream, anyway.

While I'm hanging upside down in Kansas City, Houdini has pulled off his end of the Metamorphosis. He's alive. And he's me, an eleven-year-old boy in New York City—my town—and in my century.

Houdini is in the middle of Times Square—Forty-Second Street and Broadway. You know, that spot where they drop the ball on New Year's Eve? The center of the universe.

Houdini opens his eyes and gazes up in wonder. He's been to Times Square a thousand times, but not in the 21st century. He'd seen a few skyscrapers, but nothing like the ones we have today. Now they're gigantic, surrounding him in every direction. And they all have huge signs on the side advertising movies, TV shows, and the latest Broadway musicals. Most of the signs are video screens. Houdini has never seen a video screen in his life.

Then he looks down at himself.

"I'm a boy!" he says triumphantly. "I did it!"

The streets are teeming with thousands of people, just as they are in Kansas City, yet it's so different. The men and women aren't wearing hats, as just about everybody did in Houdini's day. Some of them are wearing baseball caps, even some *women*. And they're wearing strange clothes. People are posing for pictures, but nobody is holding a camera. Or at least they're not holding the kind of camera Houdini is used to.

People are walking around dressed up like cartoon characters or giant human robots. There's a statue of the Statue of Liberty in the middle of the sidewalk. Oh, no, it isn't a statue, Houdini realizes. It's a lady *dressed* like the Statue of Liberty who is standing so still that she *looks* like a statue. Her face, arms, and legs are painted green. A man is playing a guitar and wearing nothing but underpants with NAKED COWBOY written on them.

Houdini just stares. He's as out of touch in my century as I am in his.

So much has changed since he was last in New York back in 1926. But the streets are the same, and he knows his way around. He knows where he should go. He walks east one block on Forty-Third Street. Strange-looking cars and double-decker buses clog the streets. Weird smells waft over from pushcarts with foods he's never tasted.

When he gets to the corner at Sixth Avenue,

he realizes that the elevated train tracks he remembered aren't there anymore. He looks across the street for the Hippodrome, a theater where he performed so many times.

No Hippodrome! The giant building, which once took up the whole block, is gone.

"Excuse me, ma'am," Houdini says politely to a lady passing by. "Where is the Hippodrome?"

She brushes past him without making eye contact.

Houdini assumes the lady is hard of hearing. He stops a man and asks him the same question, but the man is attending to the cell phone in his hand and barely notices anyone else. The next passerby barely slows down when Houdini approaches him.

"Sorry kid, I don't have any spare change," the guy mutters.

"I don't want change," Houdini replies, "I just want—"

But the guy walks past without turning around.

"Excuse me, ma'am," he says to the next

lady, just a little more assertively. "Where is the Hippodrome?"

"The *what?*" she replies.

"The Hippodrome," he repeats. "It was one of the largest theaters in the country. It used to be right across the street. Did it move?"

"How should I know?" the woman says brusquely before moving on. "Ask your mother. Or ask a cop."

Not a bad idea. Houdini walks down the street until he finds a policeman in the middle of the block.

"Excuse me, officer," he says, bowing slightly to show respect. "Can you direct me toward the Hippodrome? I assume the location has changed since my last visit to the city."

The policeman looks Houdini up and down carefully. All the likely possibilities go through his mind. Runaway? Lost? On drugs? Mentally challenged? Psychotic? Oddball? The boy *did* look a little out of place. But he didn't look threatening. Of course, that didn't mean he *wasn't* threatening. A lot of lunatics look perfectly normal, until they do something violent and crazy.

This personality evaluation takes about a second and a half. Finally, the policeman decides the boy in front of him is just an innocent kook.

"I heard of the Hippodrome," the cop says. "But it hasn't been here in a *long* time."

In fact, the Hippodrome closed in 1939. Houdini was right. It *had* been one of the largest theaters in the world. The stage alone was

so big, it could hold a thousand performers at a time. In its heyday, the Hippodrome was home to just about every form of popular entertainment: vaudeville, silent movies, talkies, plays, opera, boxing, wrestling, and the circus. In 1918, Houdini himself made a ten-thousand-pound elephant vanish before the audience's eyes, right on the Hippodrome stage.

Sadly, the Great Depression drove the magnificent theater out of business, and it was demolished. More than ten years went by before it was replaced by a much less glamorous twenty-one-story office building.

Houdini is sad that the site of his past glory is gone. He doesn't even notice the name of the office building that took its place.

Or the plaque right next to the reception desk inside.

Harry Houdini is not the kind of person to wallow in self-pity. He's an optimist, and he has a constant desire for adulation. If the people of the twentieth century loved him, he figures, so will the people of the 21st century. He'll just have to start all over again from scratch. No fancy props. No fame. He'll have to prove himself again. He will persist, and he will persevere. And he welcomes the challenge.

The Hippodrome isn't the only game in town. It is in the middle of the theater district. There are sure to be plenty of places for him to perform.

Houdini walks back down Forty-Third Street to the first theater he comes to—Henry Miller's Theatre. He's relieved to see it's still

THE HIPPODROME
CIRCA 1908

THE ORIGINAL HIPPODROME WAS BUILT ON
THIS SITE AS A THEATER IN 1905 BY WELL-KNOWN
SHOWMEN FRED THOMPSON AND SKIP DUNDEE.
WITH A CAPACITY OF 5,200, IT WAS THE LARGEST
AND ONE OF THE MOST SUCCESSFUL THEATERS OF
ITS TIME. THE HIPPODROME WAS KNOWN FOR
ITS LAVISH SPECTACLES AND OPULENT SETS, WHICH
INCLUDED CIRCUS ANIMALS, DIVING HORSES
AND 500-MEMBER CHORUSES. THE MOST POPULAR
VAUDEVILLE ARTISTS OF THE DAY, INCLUDING
ILLUSIONIST HARRY HOUDINI, PERFORMED AT THE
HIPPODROME. THE HIPPODROME HOSTED ITS LAST
SHOW IN 1939. CONSTRUCTION OF THE CURRENT
OFFICE BUILDING BEGAN IN 1951, WITH THE TOWER
ADDED IN 1962. SIGNIFICANT ARCHITECTURAL
DESIGN IMPROVEMENTS WERE COMPLETED IN 2006.

PHOTO COURTESY MUSEUM OF THE CITY OF NEW YORK

there, even though the big sign in front has
a name he has never heard of: Stephen Sond-
heim. Houdini strides boldly into the box
office.

"Excuse me," he says to the woman behind

the window. "Who would I speak to about booking acts?"

"Acts?" she asked.

"I do a little magic," Houdini said modestly, "and escapes, mostly. Card tricks. Pretty much anything. Much like the great Harry Houdini used to. Have you ever heard of him?"

"Sure I heard of him," the lady replied. "But we don't put on acts here. We put on plays and musicals."

Houdini smiles, pleased that his name is still remembered after so many years.

"Is there a theater where people might go to see a magician these days?" he asks.

"Uh…Madison Square Garden?" she says after thinking it over.

"Yes, of course," Houdini says, brightening. "I've been to the Garden many times. It's still around?"

"Sure it's still around," the lady replies. "Where's it gonna go?"

"Then I am off to Madison Square Park," says Houdini, tipping an imaginary hat. "On Madison Avenue, of course."

The lady snorts, as if only a total idiot would think Madison Square Garden was near Madison Square Park or Madison Avenue.

"Madison Square Garden is at Thirty-First Street," she tells him. "Between Seventh and Eighth Avenues. It's above Penn Station."

They moved the theater and put it on top of the train station? Houdini wonders silently. *How did they pull that off?*

"Aha, thank you, ma'am," Houdini says. He turns south, walking down Broadway. Hundreds of people pass by him, none giving him a second glance.

That wouldn't have happened in my day, Houdini thinks. *I was one of the most recognizable faces in the world. People would be stopping to shake my hand and ask for an autograph. I used to be the great Harry Houdini. And I will be again.*

There would be no point in telling the passersby who he is. Not yet. They would just laugh in his face. He would have to prove himself first.

Forty-First Street...Thirty-Ninth Street.

He knows he's heading in the right direction. A hot dog vendor is on the corner, and the smell makes Houdini feel a little hungry. He digs into his pockets and is relieved to find some coins.

"How much?" he asks the hot dog man.

"Four bucks."

"Four bucks?!" exclaims Houdini. "Are you out of your mind? In my day, a hot dog was a nickel."

"Then go back to your day, buddy," the vendor mutters without looking up.

Thirty-Seventh Street...Thirty-Fifth Street. A newsstand has a row of newspapers on display and Houdini scans the headlines as he walks by. LUNATIC STABS LAWYER IN BAR BRAWL. Houdini shakes his head. Some things never change.

Thirty-Fourth Street...Thirty-Second Street. He wonders where all the cigar stores and furriers went. Now every few blocks has something called Starbucks, whatever that is. Or a dry cleaner. A pizza joint. A homeless man sleeping on the street. Another one begging for money. Eyebrow threading? What could *that* be?

Finally, he sees the sign for Madison Square Garden. The building is huge, much bigger than the one he remembers. The sign is another one of those video screens, flashing a different performance every five seconds: New York Knicks vs. Boston Celtics...

Monster Truck Show...a series of rock bands and rappers. Houdini has never heard of any of them.

He marches through the front doors confidently until he encounters a burly-looking man, with his thick arms crossed in front of him.

"This area is off-limits, sonny," says the unsmiling security guard.

"My good man," Houdini says, turning on the charm. "Who is in charge of booking acts at Madison Square Garden?"

"Don't touch me, kid," replies the security guard. "Get outta here."

Houdini backs off. He has heard that word before, but it had never been directed at him.

"My apologies," he says. "Perhaps a small demonstration of my skill will improve your disposition."

He reaches into his pocket and pulls out a small box of needles. He puts a bunch of them in his mouth and pretends to swallow them. Then he does the same thing with a long thread. He waits a moment, then reaches into his mouth and pulls out the thread with needles dangling from it. The East Indian Needle Trick!

The security guard is unimpressed.

"Get out of my face, punk," he says.

Houdini takes a deck of cards out of his pocket and does a fancy shuffle.

"Pick a card," he says. "Any card."

The security guard refuses to pick a card. "I've seen David Copperfield, kid," he tells Houdini. "He made the Statue of Liberty disappear. So beat it."

You can't win 'em all. If at first you don't succeed, and so on. Houdini bows politely and wishes the man well. He leaves the Garden and walks back uptown on Eighth Avenue, lost in his thoughts. He doesn't have the expensive props he would need to do the Water Torture Cell trick or one of the other elaborate escapes from his stage act. There must be some other way he can attract attention to himself to get into the newspapers the way he did in the good old days. That is, when he was last alive.

He's thinking these thoughts as he turns right on Thirty-Fifth Street and steps off the curb. That's when a food delivery guy on an electric bike swerves around the corner.

"Watch out!" somebody shouts.

Houdini looks left at the last moment, just in time to dive out of the way, but not quick enough to avoid being smacked by the handlebar, spun around, and knocked to the ground.

"Abre los ojos, idiota!" the delivery guy shouts, which of course means "Open your eyes, idiot!" in Spanish.

A few people gather around to help Houdini get up and back on the sidewalk. He touches his face. His nose is scraped and bloody. A man offers him a napkin for his wound and a woman hands him a quarter out of pity.

"There's a shelter down the street from here," she says. "You can get a hot meal there too, I think. Do you know where your mom and dad are?"

Houdini thanks the people who helped him and brushes himself off.

This is going to be harder than I thought, he mutters to himself as he continues down Thirty-Fifth Street.

Things are not looking good. Even the great Harry Houdini is beginning to have doubts about his prospects in 21st century New York. But suddenly a wide smile spreads across his face when he sees a sign in front of him on the sidewalk.

Yes! They've created a whole museum in my memory! Houdini thinks to himself. *They still remember The Great Houdini!*

He dashes inside and takes the elevator to the fourth floor. It opens to a room with posters, photos, letters, and other mementos from his long career. Houdini looks at them for a few minutes and then marches up to the counter, where a young woman is shuffling a deck of cards.

"Do you know who I am?" he asks anxiously.

"No," she says. "What happened to your face? You're bleeding pretty bad, kid. Somebody beat you up?"

"Never mind that," he says impatiently. "I had a slight mishap on the street. The important thing is that I am Houdini! I'm alive!"

"Great, and I'm the queen of England,"

the woman says. "What can I do for you? You wanna buy a magic kit or something?"

"Don't you understand?" Houdini asks. "It's me! I said if there was a way for me to come back after I died, I would do it. Well, there is a way, and I did it! I am back!"

The woman was not impressed.

"You're going to drip blood on the counter," she said. "You should go to a hospital. Do your parents know where you are?"

"Don't you grasp the enormity of what is right in front of your eyes?" Houdini implores the woman. "I pulled off the greatest Metamorphosis ever!"

"Congrats," she says sarcastically. "Kid, nuts come in here all the time saying they're the next Houdini."

"But I really *am* Houdini!" Houdini yells at her. "I need your help to get some bookings so I can prove I am who I say I am."

The other people in the museum turn to see what's going on. As the woman behind the counter reaches into her pocket for her cell phone, a guy in a football jersey approaches Houdini.

"I'm going to have to ask you to leave, son," he says. "You're disturbing the other visitors."

"If I were not Houdini, would I be able to do *this*?" he says, reaching into his pocket and pulling out a needle. He proceeds to poke it through his cheek. Everybody in the museum gasps. The woman behind the counter dials 911 on her cell phone.

"Whoa, calm down, kid," says the guy in the football jersey. "There's no need to do that. We'll get you the help you need."

Not more than a minute later, two cops enter the museum.

"What seems to be the problem?" one of them asks.

"This young man is being disruptive, violent, and self-destructive," whispers the woman behind the counter.

"Has he got a weapon?" asks the other cop.

"He stuck a needle through his own face," says the guy in the football jersey.

"Okay, buddy," the first cop says, grabbing Houdini by the arm. "Come with us."

"I'm Harry Houdini!" Houdini shouts. "Can't you see?"

The second cop pulls a pair of handcuffs off his belt and wraps them around Houdini's wrists.

"Handcuffs?" Houdini says, a smirk on his face. "*Really*?"

GET A LIFE

When I opened my eyes, I was lying in my bed again, just as I had been before my little straitjacket adventure in Kansas City.

First things first. I checked myself all over. I wasn't Houdini anymore. I was *me*. What a relief! My arms and shoulders were sore from struggling to get out of the straitjacket. But other than that, everything was back to normal.

I looked at the clock on my night table. Eleven o'clock. Well, at least Houdini had kept his promise. Metamorphosis had lasted exactly one hour. My mom never knew I was away. Nobody else knew what happened. No harm. It was like I had been in bed the whole time. I went back to sleep and didn't wake up again until my alarm went off at seven in the morning.

I brushed my teeth and stumbled downstairs for breakfast. My mom was already in the kitchen, getting ready for work.

"Morning," she said cheerfully. "Sleep good, Harry?"

"Yeah," I told her. "I had a dream, I think."

"Oh, what happened?"

I could have told her the whole story of the straitjacket and pretended it was a dream. But I just didn't want to get into it.

"I don't remember," I said. "It slipped away as soon as I woke up."

When I got to school, Zeke caught up to me outside the media center. The little argument we had at St. John the Divine was in the past.

Zeke and I have known each other too long to let things like that bother us.

"You won't believe what happened to me last night," he said.

"Do tell."

"My dad came home from work and he said he had a surprise for me," Zeke told me excitedly. "So he handed me this box and I opened it up. And you know what was inside?"

"What?"

"A box!" Zeke said. "So I opened up the second box and you know what was inside it?"

"Another box?" I guessed.

"Yes!" Zeke exclaimed. "And there were three more boxes, each one smaller than the one before it. My dad gave me a bunch of boxes!"

"Your dad is weird, dude," I told him.

"I know, right?" Zeke replied. "So what's going on with you?"

"You wouldn't believe me if I told you," I said.

"Try me."

I wasn't sure I wanted to get into it with Zeke. He already thought I was crazy, and what happened to me the night before was even crazier. But Zeke is my best friend. He'd do anything for me, and I'd do anything for him. So I decided to be honest.

"I switched places with Houdini," I said, checking to see if Zeke was rolling his eyes. "He calls it Metamorphosis. He sent me to Kansas City in 1921and I became him. When I got there, some guys put me in a straitjacket and hung me upside down from a building…"

I told Zeke the whole story of how I got myself free. He just stared at me with his mouth open the whole time.

"Wow," he finally said. "That was way more interesting than my dad's boxes."

"Yeah," I told him, "your story was a little lame."

Zeke took a moment to take it all in. I could tell he was trying to process everything I had said. Or maybe he was just wondering whether he should have me checked into a mental institution.

"What was it like?" he finally asked. "Being Houdini, I mean."

"I was scared to death," I admitted. "I thought I might pee in my pants. You think I'm nuts, right?"

"No, no," Zeke assured me. "But let me ask you a question. If you switched places with Houdini and you became Houdini, did he become *you*?"

"I don't know," I said. "I guess so. I had a dream that he was here, wandering around Times Square trying to find a place to do his act."

The bell rang, and we had to go to class. I told Zeke we'd talk about it later.

All day long at school, I had a bad feeling inside. Houdini was going to text me again at some point, for sure. But I didn't know when. I had left the flip phone at home because I didn't want to deal with him. I was beginning to regret ever getting the phone. It's funny, when Houdini first contacted me, I was so excited. Now I was avoiding him, like he was a telemarketer trying to sell me something.

"Mr. Mancini, did you hear the question?"

my Social Studies teacher Mrs. Ashbury suddenly asked me.

"Huh?" I said. "Yeah, I'm sorry. My mind was wandering."

"Well tell it to wander back to the Revolutionary War," she replied. "We'll have a test on this material tomorrow."

When I got home from school, I did my homework and tried to study. I didn't talk much over dinner. Afterward, I went to my room and watched some YouTube videos to take my mind off Houdini. My mom poked her head into my room.

"You okay, honey?" she asked. "You've been awfully quiet today."

"I'm fine," I replied. "I guess I'm a little nervous because I have a Social Studies test tomorrow."

"Maybe you should get to bed early tonight," she said. "I'm going to sleep now. I'll see you in the morning."

Yeah, going to bed sounded like a good idea. Maybe Houdini wouldn't call at all. Maybe he got Metamorphosis out of his system and I wouldn't hear from him again. It occurred to me that once the battery on the phone died, he wouldn't be able to contact me if he wanted to. But right now it had a full charge. It would take a few hours of solid texting to drain it.

That's when it happened.

Bzzzzz...bzzzzz...bzzzzz...

Oh no, it was *him*. I didn't want to text with him.

I let it ring a few more times, hoping it might stop. But it didn't. Reluctantly, I flipped opened the phone. This was on the screen...

"HARRY, IT'S ME, HARRY."

Of course it was him. Who else could it be?

"Yeah," I tapped.

"THAT WAS SOME METAMORPHOSIS, WASN'T IT?"

"Yeah," I tapped again. I didn't want to get into an argument about it. I was mad.

But Houdini was in a talkative mood.

"I WAS A BOY, LIKE YOU!" he texted. "IT FELT SO GOOD TO BE YOUNG AGAIN! AND THE CITY CHANGED SO MUCH! THE

CARS! THE FASHIONS! THE SKYSCRAP-ERS! I HAD A WONDERFUL TIME! AT ONE POINT I GOT ARRESTED AND THE COP HANDCUFFED ME. THEY THOUGHT THEY COULD HOLD ME WITH HAND-CUFFS! CAN YOU BELIEVE THAT?"

He went on and on, describing his adventure in New York just the way it had happened in my dream. He could barely contain his excitement.

I didn't respond. I just watched the words scroll up the screen. It didn't seem to register in his mind that I was angry.

"SO HOW DID YOU LIKE BEING THE GREAT HOUDINI?" he finally asked.

I didn't reply. If you don't have something nice to say, don't say anything at all. That's what my mom always tells me.

"YOU STILL THERE, HARRY?"

"Yeah," I tapped.

"SOMETHING WRONG?"

I decided to be honest.

"Yes, something is wrong," I tapped. "You deceived me."

"HOW?"

He didn't have a clue. It was like he didn't pick up on other people's feelings.

"How do you think?" I tapped. "I could have been killed."

"BUT YOU SAID YOU WANTED TO BE FAMOUS," Houdini texted. "I SAID I WOULD MAKE YOU THE MOST FAMOUS MAN IN THE WORLD FOR ONE HOUR, AND THAT'S EXACTLY WHAT I DID."

"You didn't tell me I'd have to hang upside down and get out of a straitjacket!" I tapped angrily. "You did a misdirection on me!"

"YOU WANTED TO BE FAMOUS, HARRY," he continued. "FAME DOESN'T JUST HAP-PEN TO PEOPLE. YOU HAVE TO DO SOME-THING TO GET FAMOUS."

In the 21st century, it occurred to me, people can become famous overnight by simply put-ting on some silly costume or by posting an outrageous tweet that goes viral. In Houdini's day, you had to actually *do* something amaz-ing to get famous. And after you did it, there was no Internet to spread the word about what you did. They didn't even have *television* yet. Houdini had to risk his life escaping from something every day, in every town, in front of a live audience. And the people must have felt they had to make the effort to *be* there to see it in person. Because they never knew when he might fail to escape, or even die trying.

Still, I was mad. He should apologize.

"You should have warned me," I tapped. "That would have been the right thing to do."

"BUT ADMIT IT," he texted. "YOU HAD FUN, DIDN'T YOU?"

"Fun?" I tapped. "I wouldn't call it fun. Maybe it's fun for you to put your life on the line. It wasn't fun for me."

"BUT YOU GOT OUT OF THE STRAIT-JACKET, RIGHT?" he texted. "YOU ESCAPED."

"Yes."

"AND YOU CONFRONTED YOUR FEAR OF HEIGHTS."

"I had no choice."

"AND I BET IT MADE YOU A BETTER PERSON," he texted. "NOW YOU KNOW

THAT IF YOU COULD ESCAPE FROM THAT SITUATION, YOU CAN ACCOMPLISH ANYTHING."

"Maybe."

"AND I'LL BET YOU LIKED HEARING ALL THOSE PEOPLE CHEERING FOR YOU."

"Yes." I had to admit I enjoyed it when I threw off the straitjacket and the crowd went crazy.

"AND YOU GAVE THOSE PEOPLE HOPE THAT THEY COULD ESCAPE FROM THE PROBLEMS IN THEIR LIVES."

"I suppose."

"SO ALL IN ALL, METAMORPHOSIS WAS A GOOD THING FOR YOU, AGREE?"

Maybe it was. I don't know. I was just glad it was over. He was a jerk.

I thought that would be the end of it. I didn't want to communicate with Harry Houdini anymore. He had tricked me, and I didn't like being tricked. I had been living a perfectly happy life before he entered it. I didn't need so much stress and excitement in my life.

I tried to think of a way to end the conversation.

"I'm pretty tired" I began tapping, when his next text came in.

"HARRY," he texted. "THERE'S SOMETHING I NEED TO TALK TO YOU ABOUT."

Oh no. Here it comes. What was he going to do *now*? Have me locked in a trunk and thrown in a river?

"What is it?" I tapped, fearing the worst.

"I WANT TO DO ANOTHER METAMORPHOSIS."

"No," I tapped right away. "You're joking, right?"

"HEAR ME OUT," he went on. "THIS TIME, YOU DON'T HAVE TO DO AN ESCAPE. YOU DON'T HAVE TO RISK YOUR LIFE. YOU DON'T EVEN HAVE TO BE HOUDINI. YOU CAN BE YOURSELF."

"What would I have to do?" I tapped.

"WHATEVER YOU WANT," he texted. "WE WILL SWITCH PLACES AGAIN, BUT YOU CAN JUST BE A REGULAR PERSON."

I'm already a regular person, and perfectly happy living in my own time. I don't need to go back to "the good old days." The good old days didn't seem all that good to me. But I didn't want to make him angry.

"What's in it for you?" I tapped.

"DID YOU EVER HEAR OF REINCARNATION?" he replied.

"Yes," I tapped, although I really wasn't quite sure what the word meant.

"I GET TO LIVE AGAIN."

"Being alive for an hour means that much to you?" I asked.

"NO," he texted. "BEING ALIVE PERMANENTLY MEANS THAT MUCH TO ME."

He *had* to be joking. He couldn't be serious. He wanted to do Metamorphosis with me... forever?

"I'm not going to live in your century," I tapped. "My mother is here. My friends. My school."

"YOU CAN BRING YOUR MOTHER ALONG," he texted. "SHE WILL LOVE IT."

I didn't have to think it over. It was a ridiculous idea.

"No thank you," I tapped.

There was a very long pause, while I waited for him to reply. I thought that maybe my phone battery had died. Wishful thinking. I checked the charge, and it was over fifty percent.

"THIS IS NOT AN OFFER," he finally texted. "HARRY, WE ARE GOING TO DO THIS."

I felt the hairs on my arms going up. He wrote it in a way I didn't like, like this decision was entirely his, and his alone. Like it was out of my control. But maybe I was just misinterpreting his words.

"What do you mean?" I tapped.

"JUST WHAT I SAID," he texted back. "WE ARE GOING TO DO THIS."

"You say that like I'm not part of the decision," I tapped.

"YOU AREN'T."

I was in trouble, I realized. Big trouble. Houdini had power over me. He knew I was afraid of heights, so he had me hung from a tall building. He knew I was afraid of bullies, and now he was bullying me.

My mind was racing. The first time we did Metamorphosis, I didn't have to do anything. I just lay there on my bed. It was all him. Could he actually do it a second time, but against my will? I was starting to panic.

"Metamorphosis is over," I tapped. "Let's go back to our own lives."

"THAT'S EASY FOR YOU TO SAY," Houdini texted back. "YOU HAVE A LIFE. I'M STUCK HERE IN ETERNITY."

"That's really not my problem," I tapped.

"NO, BUT YOU ARE MY SOLUTION."

"I'm not doing it," I tapped. "I have free will."

"YOU DON'T SEEM TO UNDERSTAND, HARRY," he texted. "I CHOSE YOU. I AM IN CONTROL."

"Why me?" I tapped as fast as my fingers could move. "Pick somebody else. I bet there are a lot of people in my century who would be happy to switch places with you and go back to the 1920s. Why don't you pick somebody who's unhappy in my time and would love for nothing more than to escape from the 21st century?"

"I'M SORRY," he texted back. "BUT THIS IS THE WAY IT'S GOING TO BE."

"You're sorry? This is a funny way of showing it."

"YOU MUST UNDERSTAND SOME-THING," he texted. "WHEN I WANT SOME-THING, I GET IT. THAT'S ONE OF THE NICE THINGS ABOUT BEING FAMOUS."

This was not fair. He was an egomaniac. Why had it taken me so long to realize that? I thought he just wanted somebody to talk to.

"And what if I don't cooperate?" I texted.

"I DON'T NEED YOUR COOPERATION, HARRY."

"I thought you were a good guy."

"I'M A DESPERATE GUY. DESPERATE MEN DO DESPERATE THINGS."

I was a desperate guy too. The difference was that I was powerless.

Houdini was right about one thing. Every-body wants to escape from where they are. How was I going to escape from where I was?

"Wait a minute," I tapped desperately. "You played me! You knew everything about me from the beginning, didn't you? When you were asking me who I was and where I lived, you knew all that stuff already, didn't you?"

"OF COURSE," he texted back. "I MAY BE DEAD, BUT I'M NOT AN IDIOT. I NEEDED SOMEBODY TO SWITCH PLACES WITH ME, AND I FOUND YOU."

"You're evil!"

"HARRY, I AM A REASONABLE MAN," Houdini texted. "I WILL GIVE YOU ONE HOUR TO PACK A SUITCASE AND SAY GOODBYE TO YOUR LOVED ONES."

I didn't know what to do. Sweat was pouring down my face. I closed the phone and hung up on him.

BACK ON TRACK

I looked around my bedroom frantically, as if a simple solution to my problem was sitting on the bookcase. But there was no solution.

It was eleven o'clock, according to the clock on my night table. I made a mental note. At midnight, Houdini was going to do another Metamorphosis on me. I didn't know what to do. What were my options? None. I didn't have any.

I was going to have to tell my mom about the whole thing.

No, I couldn't do that. Anyway, she was sleeping.

Zeke! Zeke would know what to do.

I slipped the flip phone into my pocket and tiptoed out of my bedroom, being careful not to step on the creaky floorboard and wake up my mother. I felt my way in the dark to the kitchen, where our landline phone is on the wall. I dialed Zeke's cell number. It took three or four rings until he picked it up.

"Hullo?" he muttered.

"Zeke, I'm in big trouble," I whispered quickly. "I don't know what to do. I need your advice."

"What?" he mumbled. "I was sleeping. It's late. What are you doing up? What's so important?"

"I know you think I'm crazy, and I'm making all this up," I whispered. "But you're my best friend and I have nobody else to turn to. I was texting with Houdini again, and he's out of control. He wants to do another Metamorphosis."

"Huh?" Zeke asked. "A *what*? What are you talking about?"

"He wants to switch places with me again … but this time permanently!"

"So tell him no," Zeke replied. "Problem solved."

"I did! He doesn't care! He's just going to do it"—I glanced at the clock on the wall—"in fifty-six minutes, whether I want to or not!"

I told Zeke the story as quickly as I could and asked him what I should do. He thought it over for a few seconds. It seemed like he had shaken off the fog of sleep.

"Okay," he said. "Meet me at Riverside Park as soon as you can get there."

"*Where* in Riverside Park?" I asked.

"The Freedom Tunnel," he replied. "And bring the phone."

I grabbed a flashlight from a drawer and snuck out of the house, closing the front door as quietly as possible. My mother would be furious if she discovered that I went out in the middle of the night without her permission. But I had no other choice.

The street was empty except for a homeless guy sleeping on a bench near the corner of 113th Street. I looked both ways before crossing the street. All I needed was to get hit by a bike or electric scooter in the middle of the night.

I wasn't going to risk climbing up all those steps through Morningside Park in the dark. It would be too dangerous. Instead, I walked a few blocks out of my way to take the longer route along 110th Street. That ate up valuable time, but 110th is a major street and there are lights there.

I rushed across Broadway and then Riverside Drive to get to Riverside Park. It took a few more minutes to find the entrance we had used to get to the Freedom Tunnel.

Zeke wasn't there yet. I checked the time on the cell phone. It was 11:20. I only had forty minutes left until Houdini was going to do the Metamorphosis to me.

"Where *is* he?" I muttered to myself. I was sweating all over.

Finally Zeke showed up, all out of breath. He was still in his pajamas.

"I didn't have time to put on pants," he explained. "Do you have the phone?"

I took it out of my pocket.

"There's only one solution to your problem," he said. "We've got to destroy this thing. Not just destroy it. We've gotta bust it up so badly that it's beyond repair. Render it inoperable. So he'll *never* be able to contact you again. Are you gonna be okay with that?"

"Yeah," I said, "I have no other choice."

I went to pull open the big gate, but Zeke stopped me.

"Wait," he said.

"What?"

"Tuck your laces inside your sneakers," Zeke said, "so they won't get caught on the track this time."

Good thinking. While I retied my shoes, Zeke went over to the gate and yanked it open. Luckily, nobody had put a lock on since the last time we were there.

We went inside the tunnel. It smelled bad. Probably a squirrel or some other animal had died in there. Or for all I knew it was a live animal. Either way, it stunk. And it was creepy. I was glad I had a flashlight.

Zeke put his ear against the track.

"I don't hear anything," he said.

"The trains probably don't run very frequently at this time of night," I told him. "What if a train doesn't come until after midnight?"

"Then this was the stupidest thing we've ever done," Zeke replied. "How much time do you have left?"

I checked the flip phone. "Thirty-five minutes."

Zeke sat down on the track and pulled out his cell phone.

"What are you doing?" I asked.

"Checking the train schedule," he replied. "I should have done this before I told you to come here."

It took him a couple of minutes to get online

and pull up the train schedule. I paced back and forth nervously.

"We may be in luck," he finally reported. "It says there's a train leaving Penn Station at 11:45. It should take about ten minutes to get here. That's 11:55."

We would be cutting it close. But there was nothing else we could do at this point. I sat down on the track next to Zeke and waited. It felt like forever.

"So," I said, "do you believe me? About Houdini, I mean?"

"Of course I believe you," he replied. "He sounds like a strange guy."

"He was so nice to me," I said. "At least in the beginning. Then he showed what he was really like. That's when I realized what he *really* wanted."

"What did he want?" Zeke asked.

"He wanted to pull off the ultimate escape," I said. "He wanted to escape from his own death."

Zeke shook his head.

"The problem was," I continued, "he wanted

to use *me* to do it. But I'm happy where I am. I don't want to go to his time and live there forever."

"You're not going to," Zeke assured me. He checked his cell phone. It was ten minutes until midnight.

"The train should have already left Penn Station," I said.

"It may be running late," Zeke said as he got off the rail and put his ear to the track again. "I didn't think about that."

Sweat was starting to accumulate on my forehead. I wiped it away with my sleeve.

"Wait a minute!" Zeke said suddenly. "I think I feel something."

I put my ear against the track too. I could feel a faint vibration, but I didn't know if that was normal.

"I hear it!" Zeke said. "Quick! It's coming. Put the phone on the track!"

I could hear it too. I put the flashlight on the ground and placed the phone on the track. But it slid off. The phone was so much bigger than the coins we had flattened the first time, and the track was only a few inches wide.

"Hurry up!" Zeke said. "The train will be here any minute!"

"I'm *trying*!" I replied.

I put the phone on the track sideways, but it slid off again. The track was vibrating, which made it harder to keep the phone in one place. I wished I had brought some tape or glue or something to hold it on the track. Too late now.

"It won't stay!" I shouted.

"Let *me* do it!" Zeke said frantically.

But he couldn't do it either. The phone kept sliding off the track. While Zeke was on his hands and knees, I looked up. There were two lights coming toward us in the distance.

"I see it!" I said. "Try again!"

Zeke cursed. The phone slipped off the track again.

"What are we gonna do?" I asked.

The lights were getting closer. I probably had less than thirty seconds left.

"Forget this idea," Zeke said, picking up my

phone. "It's not going to work. You could lose your hand."

I looked up. I could see the train now. My heart was racing. In about ten seconds the train would be right on top of us. I could barely hear Zeke shouting at me.

"Okay, here's what we're gonna do," he hollered, handing me the phone. "When the train goes by, toss it under the wheels!"

"What, are you crazy?" I shouted. "Why me?"

"It's your phone!" Zeke shouted. "You gotta do it."

"What if I miss?"

"Then you miss," Zeke shouted. "Enjoy your new life in the Roaring Twenties."

The train was bearing down on us. It was so loud. I couldn't communicate with Zeke anymore. He backed away and covered his ears with his hands.

The train seemed like it was right on top of me. I crouched down as it rushed by and tossed the phone underhand into the wheels.

I'm not sure what happened after that. I couldn't see the phone as it disappeared into the darkness. But I heard a cracking sound when the case shattered, then I saw sparks. Bits of plastic and metal went flying all over. Some of them hit my arms and legs. I put my hands up to protect my face as I dove out of the way, stumbling backward and landing on the rocks next to the tracks. I banged my head against something hard.

And that's all I remember.

GOING HOME

But when I opened my eyes, I remembered *everything*.

I could picture every little detail of what had happened leading up to that moment. The headlights. The noise. The train coming right at us. The crunching sound, and the sparks that flew after I tossed the cell phone onto the tracks. I remembered diving out of the way and banging my head. It was so clear.

And just like the first time I woke up after my little adventure at the train tracks, I had a headache and my throat was sore. I felt sore all over. And once again, when I woke up, my mom was holding my hand.

"He's awake!" she screamed. "Harry woke up! It's a miracle! Nurse! Nurse!"

As my mother was hugging and kissing me, I looked behind her at the room. I was in the hospital again. It was a different room, but it had pretty much the same kind of machines and stuff as the first time. Flowers, cards, and candy boxes were strewn all over the window-sill. I had an IV and various tubes going in and out of me. But I didn't seem to have any broken bones or other serious injuries.

"Where am I?" I asked.

"Roosevelt Hospital," my mother replied, tears of joy streaming down her face. "You were in a coma."

"Again?"

My mom looked at me like she didn't know what I was referring to.

A nurse came running in. She gave me

a big smile and greeting. She looked at the machines and jotted something down on a clipboard.

"How long was I in a coma?" I asked.

"Almost a week," my mother said, wiping her eyes. "I didn't think you were coming back. I thought I lost you."

"Your mom was in here with you the whole time," the nurse told me. "I don't think she ever left. She's amazing."

"I'm sorry, Mom," I told her.

I felt like I was going to cry too, for all I put her through. We're supposed to learn from our mistakes, right? My mom didn't seem mad that I had done such a stupid thing a second time. She just looked so grateful that I was alive.

"I'm just glad you're here!" she said, squeezing me. And then she started crying again.

A doctor came in. He was tall, and his nametag said DR. MINUTOLI on it.

"Well, if it isn't Rip Van Winkle!" he said cheerfully as he shook my hand. "I'm so happy to see you awake, Mr. Mancini. I bet the other doctors five bucks that you would come out of it today. You made me money."

I liked this doctor better than the one I saw the first time I came out of a coma. Dr. Minutoli put his hand on my head and felt around up there.

"The swelling is down considerably," he said. "That's good. So it's unlikely that your head is going to explode. How are you feeling?"

"Weird," I told him.

"That's normal," he explained. "I would be concerned if you *didn't* feel a little weird after being in a coma."

The doctor shined a light in my eyes.

"Harry, can you spell chrysanthemum?" he asked.

"Uh...no," I told him.

"Good," he replied, winking at me. "Nobody can. You're perfectly normal. Are you hungry?"

"Yes!"

"Get this boy something to eat!"

He told the nurse to remove my tubes and wrote something on the clipboard before he got up to leave.

"I guess I still have to stay here for a night?" I asked, as the nurse pulled out my IV.

"Just one," Dr. Minutoli said, "For observation. Then do yourself a favor and take it easy for a few weeks. And stay away from the railroad tracks."

"I'm never going back there again, I promise," I told him.

"Good. I don't ever want to see your face again. And if you start vomiting when you get home, go to another hospital. That stuff grosses me out."

The next morning, before I could check out of the hospital, they had to prepare a bunch of paperwork. The nurse said it could take a half hour. I propped myself up in the bed. My mom put a pillow behind me and used the remote control to make the top of the bed go up. Then she picked up some of the get-well cards people had sent me. We were looking at the cards together when there was a soft knock on the door. It was Zeke.

"Remember me?" he asked cautiously. When I smiled, he came in and gave me a high five.

"I don't know where you would be right now if not for Zeke," my mother told me.

I wouldn't be in a hospital, I knew *that*. It was Zeke's idea to go to the railroad tracks both times. But I didn't say that. I didn't want to get Zeke in trouble, and I didn't want my mother to know anything about the cell phone.

Zeke and I looked at each other, sending a silent message to talk it over when my mom wasn't around.

"You are so lucky," Zeke told me. "You got to miss a whole week of school. And everybody's gonna be treating you like a big hero when you get back."

"Oh yeah," I said sarcastically. "It's great to be in a coma. Really clears your head. Everybody should have one."

My mom pulled out her cell phone and took a picture of me. Then she took a picture of Zeke and me together.

"I'm going to go to the waiting room and tell everybody the good news," she said as she picked up her purse. "I'll be back in a few minutes."

As soon as she walked out the door, I turned to Zeke.

"Okay, what happened?" I asked him. "I need to know everything. Tell me the truth."

"Everything?"

"Yeah, everything."

"It was a really stupid thing to do," Zeke told me. "We were in the Freedom Tunnel down by the railroad tracks in Riverside Park. For some reason, the gate was open. So I said we should put some coins on the track to flatten them. Then, just as the train was coming, your shoelace got caught in the track. You couldn't get it loose. At the last second, you dove out of the way and hit your head. And you've been in here ever since. I'm really sorry, man. I never should have suggested we do that. It was all my fault. I'm just glad you're okay. I don't know what I would have done if you didn't wake up. And for what? For this..."

Zeke reached into his pocket and pulled out a couple of flattened coins. He handed them to me.

"That's *it*?" I asked. "That's all that happened?"

"Well, yeah."

"What about the *second* time we went to the railroad tracks?" I asked.

"Second time?" Zeke said, puzzled.

"What about the phone, Zeke?" I asked.

"What phone?"

"The *cell* phone!" I told him. "The flip phone!"

"Flip phone?" Zeke asked. "Dude, I don't know what you're talking about."

I closed my eyes for a moment to clear my head. How could he not remember that we went back to the railroad tracks and crushed the cell phone I had been using to communicate with Houdini?

"Hey, are you okay, Harry?" Zeke asked. "Are you gonna be able to come to my birthday party? It's gonna be cool. We're going to an escape room."

"What?!" I said, alarmed. "I already *went* to your birthday party at the escape room. Don't you remember?"

"Harry, it hasn't happened yet," Zeke told me. "My birthday is on Thursday."

He pointed to a calendar on the wall. The days I was in a coma had been crossed out with red marker.

"This *coming* Thursday?" I asked. Zeke nodded his head.

I had to sort it all out. Everything seemed a little foggy. The doctor had told me I might be confused a little bit at first.

"You mean...none of it happened?" I asked Zeke.

"None of *what* happened?"

"Houdini!" I said. "The flip phone! The text messages! I was hanging upside down in Kansas City and I had to get out of a straitjacket. I told you all about it, Zeke! Don't you remember Metamorphosis?"

"Meta-*what*?" Zeke replied. "Harry, you're scaring me. Are you sure you're okay?"

"So I never communicated with Houdini?" I asked.

"Dude, you didn't communicate with *anybody*," Zeke insisted. "You've been out cold for a week."

"You mean the last time I was awake was

when we flattened these coins on the train track?" I asked.

"Yes! That's what I've been trying to tell you."

This whole thing was blowing my mind.

"But it seemed so real," I finally said.

"I think you need to rest," Zeke replied.

When my mom came back to the room, she took more pictures and kept hugging me like she didn't want to let me go.

"Are you okay, Harry?" she asked. "You look a little pale. Should I call the doctor?"

"I just need to sit here for a minute," I told her.

A lady knocked on the door and told my mom they would release me from the hospital as soon as she signed some paperwork. While she did that, Zeke collected up all the flowers so they could be given to other patients on the floor. I got dressed and then picked up the boxes of candy on the windowsill. As I was stuffing them into my backpack, one of the boxes fell on the floor.

I bent down to pick it up. It was a small

box, about six inches by four inches. There was a red ribbon around it, but it was loose so it slipped off. I figured that after all I had been through, I deserved a piece of candy.

I opened the box.

No candy.

There was a cell phone inside.

FACTS & FICTIONS

Everything in this book is true, except for the stuff I made up. It's only fair to tell you which is which.

First of all, Harry Houdini was a real person, of course, and arguably the most famous celebrity of the early twentieth century. He started out as a magician, but became more famous for his ability to escape from virtually anything. Metamorphosis was a signature escape that Harry and his wife Bess performed all over the world for many years.

I researched this book mainly by reading lots of books about Houdini, such as *Houdini!!!: The Career of Erich Weiss* by Kenneth Silverman, *The Secret Life of Houdini: The Making of America's First Superhero* by William Kalush and Larry Sloman, *Houdini: The Man Who Walked Through Walls* by William Lindsay Gresham, and *The Magician and the Spirits: Harry Houdini and the Curious Pastime of Communicating with the Dead* by Deborah Noyes, to name a few. I also visited the Houdini Museum in New York City (houdini museumny.com), and watched newsreel footage and several silent movies Houdini starred in (available as Houdini: The Movie Star, a box set). If you want to know more about the man, search for his name on the Internet and it will keep you busy for weeks. If you happen to be near Scranton, Pennsylvania, visit The Houdini Museum. There's also lots of Houdini memorabilia at The History Museum at the Castle in his childhood hometown—Appleton, Wisconsin. It's a few blocks from Houdini Plaza.

Finally, I spent a lot of time in Houdini's old neighborhood. He really *did* live at 278 West 113th Street in New York City. I wasn't born there, but I live just eight blocks away and I walk by Houdini's old house frequently. In fact, that's what gave me the idea for this story.

I can easily imagine Houdini climbing the stairs in Morningside Park, visiting the Cathedral of St. John the Divine, and hanging out in Riverside Park. All these locations in the story are real, as is the Freedom Tunnel (the gate is locked, I tried it), the original Hippodrome (where Houdini famously made an elephant disappear in 1918), and the current Madison Square Garden of course.

Some biographies describe Houdini as a bit of a selfish egomaniac who demanded constant attention and adulation. I wouldn't call him a bad man, but if Houdini had the chance to text from the grave and switch places with a modern-day kid in order to pull off the ultimate escape act, I suspect that he would take it.

●●●

The stuff I made up? Harry Mancini, his mother, and his friend Zeke do not exist. And make no mistake, you *cannot* communicate with dead people by text message. Don't bother trying.

However, it's absolutely true that many people believed Houdini's escapes were so amazing that he must have had supernatural powers, and that if *anybody* could come back from the dead it would be him. Houdini was fascinated by death. In the 1922 silent film *The Man from Beyond*, a character played by Houdini was brought back to life after being frozen in Arctic ice for a hundred years. In fact, Houdini promised his wife and a number of friends that if there was a way for him to communicate with them after he died, he would do it. And to this day, every Halloween, séances are held all over the world with people gathered together trying to receive some kind of a message from his spirit.

Unfortunately, Harry Houdini has not been heard from since 1926. It's true that he was punched in the stomach and died of peritonitis (an inflammation of the abdomen) nine days later, on Halloween. He was just fifty-two years old.

Houdini is buried in the Hungarian section of Machpelah Cemetery in Ridgewood, Queens. A steady stream of visitors come to pay their respects at his large stone horseshoe-shape grave site. Often they leave playing cards, coins, and handcuffs on the gravestone. In this way, his memory is kept alive. Harry Houdini may not be able to communicate from "the other side," but he will never be forgotten.

ABOUT THE AUTHOR

Dan Gutman has written many books for young readers, such as the My Weird School series, the Genius Files, the Flashback Four series, *The Kid Who Ran for President, The Million Dollar Shot, The Homework Machine,* and his Baseball Card Adventure series. Dan and his wife, Nina Wallace, live five minutes away from Harry Houdini's house in New York City. You can find out more about Dan and his books by visiting his website (dangutman.com) or following him on Facebook, Twitter, and Instagram.